2

Rock the Band

Michelle A. Valentine

Michelle A. Valentine Books

Rock the Band

(The Black Falcon Series, #1.5)

By *Michelle A. Valentine*

Michelle A. Valentine

Dedications

To the readers: Thank you for embracing the

boys of Black Falcon. All of your love and

support means more to me then you'll ever

know.

Michelle A. Valentine

Black Falcon Series

Reading Order

Rock the Heart (Black Falcon, #1)

Rock the Band (Black Falcon, #1.5)

Rock My Bed (Black Falcon, #2)

Rock the Band

Chapter 1

Light flickered across the room as the bus rolled down the highway. The constant rumble of the wheels below us comforted me as I held the woman I loved in my arms. This was finally home. Everything I needed was on this bus. Lane had finally chosen to give herself over to me and be completely mine.

I traced my fingertips over the soft skin on her bare shoulder as she rested her head against my chest. I admit I was shocked to see her in the bar earlier tonight at the end of my gig.

That Riff could be a sneaky bastard. He was always able to pull fast ones if the situation called for it.

I never expected to see Lane so soon, but he knew how much I had been suffering and took it upon himself to arrange for us to talk things out. Over the few days we were apart, after Sophie and Mike revealed they completely fucked up my life, I'd gone over everything I wanted to say to her at least a million times. How sorry I was. How it was wrong for me not to try harder to make things work between us. I should've stood up to Sophie after she tried trapping me in a relationship I didn't want for the sake of a child—a child that turned out to not even be mine.

I closed my eyes and tried not to think about that or how stupid my thought process was over the whole situation. The idea of being the best father I possibly could've been clouded every judgment I made in all the other aspects of my life, including the way I tried to keep my relationship with Lane a secret until I figured the Sophie thing out. It was wrong of me to ask that of her, and the realization hit me hard when I thought she'd left me for good.

The bus slowed down. Our driver, Jimmy, probably needed to hit the head.

Lane stirred in my arms. "Are we nearly there?"

I smiled and ran my fingers through her brown hair. "Not yet. We still have an hour or so."

Michelle A. Valentine

I couldn't wait to get her back to my place in Kentucky. I knew after she saw it, she'd finally agree to move in with me. It was the perfect spot for us. When I bought it, I was looking for someplace like my parents house on Cedar Creek Lake back in Texas. As much as I hated to admit it, I missed that place like crazy. One of the best weekends I'd had in a long time was when Lane took me home with her to our old neighborhood. Hopefully, my place would remind her of being home and safe.

She lifted her head and placed her chin on my chest. I took a lock of her brown hair and twirled it around my finger. There was odd comfort in doing that. At times, I wished it were physically possible to wrap her entire body around me like I did with her hair on my finger. It was crazy to love someone so much, I knew that, but I couldn't help it. Being around her made me want to be a better man.

Big Bertha jerked to a stop and Lane pushed her self up on the bed. She raised her arms over her head in a delicious stretch. I tucked an arm behind my head and took in the sight of her bare chest in the moonlight. I bit my lower lip as I trailed my eyes over every inch of her body. It was amazing how fucking sexy she was.

She dropped her arms into her lap and whipped her head in my direction. Her lips pulled in to a heart-stopping smile. "Why are you looking at me like that?"

I furrowed my brow but couldn't fight back my grin. "How am I looking at you?"

Lane shrugged. "I don't know, like you're studying me."

A chuckle escaped from me as I sat up with lightning speed and pulled her back down in bed with me. I brushed a few stray hairs free from her face and then traced her delicate jaw line. She really was absolute perfection.

"Maybe I am studying you."

She readjusted her head on the pillow. "Why?"

"Just wondering why you came back to me tonight? I mean, I was fully prepared to grovel to win you back, but I was just giving you space."

She sighed and brought her hand to cup my face. "I left to give you time to figure things out. You just had your entire world rocked. I didn't want to add any more drama."

This was one of the reasons I loved this woman. She actually cared about my feelings. No one had ever done that before. She was the only person who ever put me first in their life. Not even my parents did that. The only time she ever considered herself was when she left me on the dock, but she was right to do that. I never used to put her first back then, and I see now how shitty that made me. Her leaving pushed me to succeed. It drove me. In a way, I owe her thanks for that.

I leaned my head down and placed my lips on hers. "You are my world, and you're welcome to dramatize it all you want."

Her mouth turned up into a smile. "I think it's time we live drama free for a while, don't you?"

I nodded and stroked her face.

Drama free? Was there really such a thing? Life for me had always been filled with it. The only time I'd ever experienced true peace was on stage. The surge of the crowd and the heavy thump of the drums always pulled me into almost what felt like another dimension and made me forget all the bad shit in my life. It was true, I felt nearly the same way in moments like this one with Lane, but deep down I always had to fight back the fear that someday I'd fuck things up and she would decide to run from me again.

Then it hit me. I needed to make this thing between us permanent. I had to show her I meant what I said earlier at the show, that I was hers—forever.

I stared into her green eyes and made a silent promise to myself that somehow, someway, I would make this girl my wife. The mere thought of us being apart again caused an ache I didn't think I could bear. Yes, giving her my last name would rectify that fear.

Lane reached up and tapped my temple. "I know that look. What's going on in that brain of yours?"

Damn. She caught me. I wasn't prepared to tell her about the thought that had just crossed my brain. She would probably give me the speech about taking things one day at a time. I hated that fucking speech. I was ready to live in the moment—the here and now—with her. If she could only see through my eyes for a second, she would know how I felt about her. There wouldn't be a question about my motives. She would know I loved her to the depths of her soul and she would see how completely she rocked me in every way.

"You're still doing it."

I bit my lip. She wouldn't leave me alone until I gave her an answer. I knew how relentless she could be. I shrugged and replied as coolly as I could, "Just thinking about surprising you with something."

She raised a perfectly manicured eyebrow. "What kind of surprise?"

"Now, why would I ruin it by telling you?" I teased.

Lane's lips pulled into a smile. "Guess I'll have to withhold sex until you tell me."

I grabbed her around the waist and rolled her over on her back. Every inch of my body covered her nude flesh and my cock twitched at the nearness of her moist heat. I ran my right hand up her side, knowing full well the effect of me being so forward had on her. I pinned her gaze with my eyes.

She squirmed beneath me. "You're cheating!"

I licked her bottom lip. "How is this cheating?"

Her legs moved further apart and I slid my hips between them. My throbbing dick pushed against her folds. I ran my nose along her jaw and inhaled the intense scent of her hot skin. Fragrances of sweet shampoo and a mouth-watering perfume filled my nose. Every sense in my body went on complete overload by her nearness. I dragged my lips across the flesh of her neck and when she tipped her head back, letting a moan escape from her parted, pink lips, I knew she wanted what I was about to give her.

I slid my hand down her belly until it found the point where our bodies were about to connect. Only one finger glided into her, and she bucked her hips against my hand. I ground the palm of my hand against her clit, giving it the intensity she craved. She gasped and closed her eyes. The urge to taste her raged inside me, so I snaked my tongue out and licked from the base of her throat to her chin. Lane opened her eyes, grabbed both sides of my face in her hands and crushed her lips against mine. A primal need to take her, to feel her, pushed through me, and a growl rumbled in my chest.

I loved it when she was forceful with me. It turned me on instantly when I could see the need to be pleased in her green eyes. She was practically begging me to fuck her senseless.

"Noel." She said my name with a mixture of pain and desire in her voice. My breath came out in ragged spurts, and I nipped her earlobe between my teeth. The way I felt about her was crazy. It was primal and raw. I needed to connect with her in every possible way.

I circled her clit with the tip of my finger in a forceful rhythm. Her eyes rolled back and her entire body shook as she came hard against my hand. While she was still in the moment, I grabbed the base of my shaft and guided it into her, not allowing her to time to come down from her orgasm.

"Oh. God. Yes!" she cried as I plunged into her.

Knowing I was making her scream like that was nearly enough to drive me over the edge right then and there, but I held back and tried to pretend the feel of me sliding in and out of her wasn't the best fucking feeling in the world.

Her nails raked along my back all the way down to my ass, where she grabbed it with both hands as I worked in and out of her. Lane held my gaze and chewed on her bottom lip. I couldn't resist. I bent down and kissed her, grazing my teeth along that lip.

"I love you," she whispered against my mouth. "Forever."

I closed my eyes. It was the word I'd told her earlier, that I was hers forever. To hear her confirm the same feeling, it nearly caused me to choke up.

Lane must've sensed the emotion welling up inside me, because she pushed my shoulder, forcing me on my back.

I gripped her hips in both hands as she positioned herself over the head of my cock before impaling herself with it. She gasped as she took in my length to the base. Mesmerized by the sight of her, I couldn't peel my eyes away as she rocked her hips in a steady rhythm. Long strands of her brown hair cascaded down her back. She reminded me of an angel in need of her body to be worshipped.

I sat up and wrapped my arms around her and she arched against my hands. Her muscles around my cock clenched, making it nearly impossible to hold back. "Fuck, Lane."

Both of her hands found my chest as she braced herself against me and picked up speed. She enjoyed getting me off.

I cupped her right breast as I sucked her pink nipple into my mouth. My eager tongue flicked across it as she slammed down hard on me. The warmth of our connection flowed through me as I inhaled the scent of her desire. I leaned back, enjoying the ride she was taking me on. She was getting close again. I could tell. She always grabbed her own tits when she was nearly ready to come. I watched as she plucked her left nipple between her fingers before rolling it and moaning.

"You are so fucking sexy," I told her as I watched her knead her own breast.

She grinned and leaned in and kissed my lips. I splayed my fingers across her ass and encouraged her to ride me faster. Lane whimpered as she ground her clit against me with each buck of her hips. I loved that I could make her come while I was deep inside her. With other girls, I had never cared about making the sex last long. I was only looking to get off. There never was a connection with any of them. But, with Lane, it was different. Making sure she was satisfied pleased me nearly as much as letting go inside her.

"Come with me," I whispered roughly in her ear. There was nothing better than that. Mutual gratification between us simultaneously was exactly what I craved.

Lane's moaning grew louder as she rode me with determination. She was working hard, grinding her clit against my pelvis, to comply with my request. I watched under my hooded eyelids as she tipped her head back and screamed out my name as she came for the second time.

"Fuck." The sight of her letting go caused a shudder to rip through my entire body as my cock erupted, and I filled her full.

She collapsed against me, and I kissed her cheek over and over, still craving more of her. "I love you so much."

Never in my life had I loved another person as much as Lanie Vance—I knew that now more than ever. I had to figure out a way to make her mine forever.

Chapter 2

The crazy awkward silence Riff and I had struggled with for the past few months was gone now, thankfully. It was nuts how the lies of one stupid chick was nearly the demise of the one thing we had built together—this band. Black Falcon meant everything to Riff. I knew that and so did Sophie, which is probably why she concocted the plan to blame me for getting her pregnant. She knew once it got out that Mike knocked her up, brother or not, he would've been canned. We couldn't allow shit like that to fuck up our world. The band was our top priority and Sophie was smart enough to realize that and pin it on me so Mike could keep his fucking paycheck, while I took the rap. The bitch was probably hoping to bilk me out of some money along the way, too. I couldn't believe I was stupid enough to fall for her game.

"What's the score?" Riff asked as he plopped down beside me on the loveseat to watch Trip and Tyke go at it on the *Xbox*.

He handed me a beer and I twisted the cap off. "Trip is whooping his ass as usual."

"I heard that, fucker," Tyke snapped but never took his eyes off the screen on the wall in front of him. "I'm about to murder this chump."

Tyke's blonde hair hung loose around his head, while his twin brother, Trip, kept most of his black hair concealed under a black bandanna. Thank God those two tried hard to create separate identities or I would've never been able to tell them apart based on looks alone. More than anything in the world, they hated when people confused them.

Trip laughed at his brother's last remark. "You can't whip yourself out of a wet paper bag, let alone murder me."

I took a swig of my beer while those two pounded at the buttons on their controllers.

Riff cleared his throat next to me. "So things are good with you and Lanie?"

I nodded. I was pretty sure he already knew the answer to that. She'd screamed her brains out in my room during both of our sexual escapades earlier tonight. "Yeah, things are great."

I adjusted my ass in the seat. It was hard not to bust out and tell my best friends that I planned to marry her as soon as fucking possible, but I knew the twins had a lot of reservations about Lane coming on the bus in the first place. They hated drama and saw the mind-fuck I was about to experience between her and Sophie coming a mile away. They tried to stop it, but I was ready to go to war if I had to in order to get close to Lane again. Lucky for me, I had enough pull as the front man of Black Falcon to get my way. The deal with that greedy bitch, Diana Swagger, was a terrible thing to do to the band, but I had to agree in order to get Lane on my bus for two weeks.

Trip and Tyke tried like hell to talk me out of bringing her here, but eventually gave up when they figured out just how desperate I was to get Lane back. But, me announcing that I was ready to marry her so quickly after all the shit the band just went through over a woman, well, they would have a fit. And they had every right to be apprehensive about the idea, but Lane wasn't like any other girl we'd brought on this bus. She was smart and determined to be successful in her own career in marketing. She wouldn't have time to stir up drama for us, even if she wanted to.

"How long is she staying at your place?" Riff asked while he picked at the label on his bottle.

"The entire break. She's planning on catching a ride back to Texas with us when we start back on the road."

He nodded. "A week of freedom before you have to face reality, right?"

I furrowed my brow. "Reality?"

"Yeah, you know, the true test of a relationship. Distance."

I swallowed hard. I didn't want to think about being apart from her just yet. It was too hard. I missed her like crazy at the mere thought. I could only imagine what would happen to me when I had to leave her again.

I brought the bottle to my lips and let the cold beer run down my throat. That was one of the other reasons I needed to get a ring on her ringer. Commitment. I needed it from her, and I'm sure after my selfish ass had always put her second to everything in my life, she was going to need it from me, too.

Before I could say anything to about it, Lane pulled that damn rolling suitcase down the hallway. "I'm packed. Are we ready?"

I looked over at Riff, and we bumped fists. "I'll catch you later, bro. Guys." I smacked both Trip and Tyke in the back of the head while they stayed oblivious to the world.

"Damn it, Noel. You dick! You nearly got me killed," Trip whined.

I stood and downed the rest of my beer before tossing the empty bottle into the trash can. I took Lane's bag and smiled. "And they wonder why they strike out with chicks so much."

Lane giggled, and I kissed her lips.

"I heard that! Just so you know, I don't get any complaints when it comes to how I lay the pipe," Trip retorted.

Riff nudged his boot into Trip's back. "It doesn't count when you pay them."

"Jesus! For the last time I didn't know she was a fucking hooker until afterwards. I should've never told you guys."

Tyke snorted next to him. "We would've wondered where the love of your life ran off to eventually. You had to either tell us, or go broke in order to keep her around."

I laughed, grabbed Lane's hand and led her off Big Bertha. Those guys were complete idiots, but I loved them. With my mom and dad out of the picture, they were the only real family I'd known for the past four years. We shared a bond that even I couldn't really describe. A brotherhood was the closest thing I could come up with.

The minute Lane and I stepped onto the concrete, I threaded my fingers through hers. I gazed down at her and smiled. She wrapped her free hand around my forearm and leaned into me as we walked toward Kyle, the new bodyguard I hired to replace Mike.

Kyle seemed cool enough. He was a built dude, maybe even a little bigger than Mike, and he had this vibe about him, like he was ready at any moment to rip someone's head off if the situation called for it. The female fans seemed to dig him, too. They all tried to touch his shoulder-length, brown hair, but he didn't let their attention affect him too much. In the short time I'd known Kyle, one of the very first things I learned about him was the fact he was in a serious relationship with a girl named Emily—a girl who meant a lot to him. Immediately, I respected him.

Kyle opened the door to the Escalade and took Lane's bag from me. "You guys ready to get off that bus for a while?"

Lane sighed next to me. "Yes. I can't wait to see Noel's house."

Kyle crunched his brow as he opened the back of the SUV and shoved the suitcase inside. "You've never been there before? I thought you guys have been together since high school?"

I opened the door for Lane.

"We were together all through high school, but then took a bit of a break. Technically, we just got back together," Lane told him without a stutter before she hopped into the vehicle.

Her delicate phrasing of our time apart was sweet. It was as if my past didn't bother her, and that shocked me. She was so forgiving and understanding. Even though we weren't together when I was fucking around with all those other women, I still felt guilty, like I wronged her by doing that in some way. She really was too good for me. I prayed to God that she never asked me how many women I slept with since her, because I really didn't know.

I dabbled in a little in drugs over the years until Riff forced my ass into rehab a few months back. My life during that time period was a complete fucking mess. Half of it I don't remember, which is why it was so easy for Sophie to pin shit on me. I got clean just in time for Lane to walk back into my life. If I would've been strung out when we met back up, she would've never given me another shot.

I slid in next to Lane and rested my left hand on the bare skin of her thigh. I loved it when she wore jean shorts like this. The tips of my fingers drifted onto her inner leg, and I quickly moved it as I felt my dick jerk in my pants. An hour ride with a boner would not be fun. I would be tearing her clothes off the minute we were alone if it stayed that way. I threaded my fingers through hers and thought about getting to my place and showing her the dock. I was excited for her to see it.

I knew it was selfish and even demanding on my part, but I hoped once she saw it, she'd want to stay with me. That she would forget about her original plan to move to Texas with her mom and look for another marketing job. I needed her with me. I didn't realize how much I needed her until I had her back and then lost her again.

Kyle hopped into the driver's seat and slammed the door. I rattled off my address as he tapped it into the GPS before he put the motor into drive.

Butterflies thrashed around in my stomach. It was only a matter of time now until I had Lane all to myself, and I could start phase one of my plan to make her mine forever.

"You going home for the week, Kyle?" Lane asked a few minutes into our trip.

Kyle nodded. "Yeah, I have a flight scheduled in the morning. I miss my Emily like crazy. I can't wait to get home and surprise her for a couple days. Being on the road away from her is harder than I thought."

I sighed. I knew after this week I was going to be feeling the exact same way. I gave Lane's hand a little squeeze and she turned her face towards me. She bit her lip as I regarded the look in her eyes. The same thing was on her mind. I could tell because her eyes always gave her thoughts away. I reached up and tucked her hair behind her ear with my free hand. The tips of my fingers lingered on her face.

Lane leaned in and kissed my lips before she whispered, "I love you."

I tipped my head and placed my forehead against hers. "Forever."

We made small talk with Kyle the rest of the way to my place. About thirty minutes into the drive, Lane and Kyle both kept commenting about how dark it was in the middle of the Kentucky woods. I admit it could be pretty unnerving until you grew accustomed to being in the country. The band's agent hated that we lived out here. It was away from everything, including commonly used amenities. The best we could get was satellite internet and cable. And cell service, forget it, which was one of the major reasons I loved living out here. I could really get away from everything.

"Around the curve on the left is my driveway. You'll see the gate," I instructed Kyle.

We turned into the drive and Lane sat up straighter in her seat. "I can't wait to see your house."

I gave her thigh a gentle squeeze. "And I can't wait to show it to you."

Relief flooded me the minute my modest, log cabin with a lone porch light came into view. Everything still looked the same, but in the darkness, it was hard to tell. I was always taking a chance when I left the house unattended while I was on tour. Someone could rob me blind and I might not find out until months later when I came back. Everyone said I needed a security system, but way out here, I didn't think I needed it.

It was good to be home. This was the one place I could get away from my life—the one place where I felt normal. Before Lane came back to me, I felt like a piece of meat. Fans, especially the female variety, always wanted a piece of me, and they shamelessly used me for my fame.

I had been looking for a love to replace Lane's—to get her out of my head and heart, but I couldn't find anyone that ever compared to her. The women never wanted me, not really. They wanted a rock star, and most of the time they could care less if it was Riff or me they ended up sleeping with. People always called men dogs, but in reality, women were just as bad.

Kyle pulled up next to the house and cut the engine. "Wow, man. This place is secluded."

I chuckled as I opened the door. "Just the way I like it."

Kyle headed toward the trunk as I helped Lane out. "I could never live out here like this."

He stacked our luggage on the front porch. "After the crazy life I live most of the time, I love being away from it all."

Lane fixed her hands on her hips as she peered around her surroundings. "Well, I like it."

I raised my brow. "You do?"

She nodded before she turned and threw her arms around my neck. "It's peaceful and a nice change from the bus."

My hands slid around her waist, and I drew her into me. Her chest pushed against mine as I leaned down and kissed her sweet lips. "You mean you won't miss living in cramped corners with a bunch of drunk assholes?"

She giggled in my arms and shook her head. "They aren't so bad, but I am looking forward to some alone time with you."

A grin spread across my face. "Be ready, babe. Right now starts an entire week of just you and me. Speaking of which…Kyle, we're good here, man. You can head back."

Kyle shut the doors on the Escalade and pulled the keys from his pocket. "All right, then. I'll be back on Tuesday morning to pick you guys up."

Lane rested her cheek against my chest and placed her hand on my chest. "Be careful driving back."

Together we watched as Kyle drove away. The minute his taillights were out of sight, I scooped Lane into my arms.

She tossed her head back and laughed as I carried her towards the front door. "Aren't you Mr. Romance?"

The warmth of her body against mine stirred every nerve within my body. I didn't think I was ever going to get enough of this woman. After I stepped onto the porch, I tipped her up, and she planted both feet onto the ground. Lane wrapped her arms around herself and shook a little from the slight nip in the night air as I lifted the welcome mat to retrieve the key to let us inside.

She twisted her lips. "Really? Who knew mega-famous rocker, Noel Falcon, keeps a hide-a-key."

I chuckled and unlocked the front door. "The hiding place stays between us."

Before she could quip with another smart-ass remark, I lifted her back into my arms and carried her through the door.

She shook her head. "Noel, you're such an idiot. This is a tradition for newlyweds."

I shrugged. "Practice makes perfect."

After a quick peck, I set her down again and flicked on the lights. Relief flooded me. The entire place was just as I had left it. Hardwood floors throughout the cabin gleamed against the glow of the recessed lighting. The great room was clean and orderly, with each of my pillows still perfectly placed on my black-leather sofa.

Lane rubbed her hands together as he took in the layout of the room, and I closed us inside. "Do you have a housekeeper?"

I bit my bottom lip as I pulled her into me again. It was nearly impossible to keep my hands to myself around her. "Nope."

She scrunched her nose, and it was so fucking cute. I stretched my finger up and tapped it.

"You don't think I'm capable of keeping a clean house?" Her hair trailed down her back and I caught a strand of it and wrapped it around my finger.

She licked her lips and peered into my eyes. "I didn't know that was one of your many skills."

Holy hell. A naughty glint twinkled in her eyes. She was going to kill me if we kept going at this pace. Not that I was complaining. Death by sex—it would be the best fucking way to die. But, three or four times a day would definitely have me addicted to making love to her. How would I ever get anything else done? I still needed to be a functioning human being.

I grabbed the waistband of her jeans and yanked her flush against my body. "I've got enough skills to keep you surprised and satisfied for a lifetime."

She grabbed fistfuls of my hair and yanked my mouth down to hers. The warmth of her mouth sent a signal below my belt that it was time for action. Our tongues danced together while I slid my hand under her shirt. The silk of her bra was all that separated my hand from her perfect skin. I dipped my fingers inside the cup and shoved it underneath her breast. The nipple became rigid beneath my hand, and I squeezed it roughly, causing my cock to jerk hard inside my jeans.

I shoved her tank top up and bent down to take one of those perfect nipples into my mouth. She moaned and ran her fingers through my hair. And damn, if that didn't get me even more excited.

Her skin blazed beneath my lips as I kissed a trail up her chest to her lips. All of my fingers found their way into her hair as I plunged my tongue into her mouth. The fabric of my red t-shirt strained against my skin as she yanked a handful in her fists. This side of Lane turned me on more than anything. The way it seemed she couldn't get enough of me thrilled me because it mimicked the exact feeling I had for her.

I walked her backwards towards my couch, and when the back of her knees hit it, I laid her down.

I tore my shirt off my body, anxious to have the feel of her skin against every inch of me. Lane panted while peering up at me through sex-hazed eyes as I stood over her. There was nothing sexier than a woman in need of a good fucking, and right now, Lane was the sexiest fucking thing I'd ever seen.

That was the last coherent thought that flowed through my brain before I made quick work of tearing off her clothes to give her just what she needed.

Chapter 3

A soft snore was the only sound bouncing around the four familiar walls of my loft bedroom. Lane's head rested against my chest while she curled her fingers into a loose fist on my stomach. I played with a strand of her hair between my fingers as my eyes roamed over every inch of her exposed olive-toned skin. The fact she was comfortable enough to sleep practically right on top of me made me grin like an idiot. She was truly my soul mate. It was practically like we were the same person.

I wasn't sure how long I laid there and stared at her perfection, but it was long enough that the sun rose a little higher and struck my bed at the perfect angle to shine right on us.

My God, she really looked like a fucking angel. I still had a hard time believing she came back to me. She's really too good to be mine.

Lane stirred a little in my arms, and I rubbed the bare skin of her shoulders with the pads of my fingers. "Good morning, sleepy-head. Do you want breakfast?"

She snuggled tighter into me and giggled. "Mom's not here to supervise your pancake flipping skills this time."

"Hey." I nudged her a little. "I resent that. I'll have you know I've mastered the perfect pancake now."

She sat up and pulled the quilt around her chest before swinging her legs over the side of the bed.

The bed suddenly felt colder without her in it. "Where are you going? Come back."

She shook her head. "Oh, no. I have to see the master of pancake making in action."

I sat up in bed and pulled her back against my chest. I kissed the soft skin on her neck while I inhaled the scent of her fruity shampoo mixed with her perfume. "Are you sure you don't want to come back to bed?"

I continued to tease her and allowed my lips to linger at the pressure point just below her ear. She cocked her head to the side, giving me better access, while she squirmed against me. This newly found little area seemed to be the spot of her undoing. Every time I went for it, she went a little crazy, which in turn, excited me even more.

"Please come back to bed?" I whispered roughly, as I ran my hands up her sides before reaching around and slipping her breast into my palms. "Please?"

I knew it seemed crazy to crave someone so much, but I couldn't help it. I was fucking addicted to her.

"Noel…" The way she said my name made me bite the inside of my lower lip. It was rough and slightly breathless. I knew she wouldn't be resisting me too much longer. She enjoyed sex just as much as I did. Hell, she liked it so much she forgot to eat half the time.

"Come on. A morning quickie, then I promise to keep my hands to myself until tonight."

She whipped her head towards me and raised an eyebrow. "You? Keep your hands to yourself? Sounds like an easy bet I'd be able to win."

A grin tugged at my lips. She was right. I probably wouldn't be able to keep my hands off her completely, but I'd be damned if I let her see just how much of an effect she had on my self-control. Damn it. I needed to keep some fucking man cards here.

"Careful, you're opening yourself up to a dangerous situation. I don't think *you* can go an entire day without touching me either," I quipped right back at her.

She turned to face me while still holding the blanket tight around her chest. "I think I can."

I tilted my chin and stared down at her. "You do, do you?"

Lane nodded with a smug smile. "Absolutely."

The stubble along my jaw was rough as I ran my hand across it. "I say we make a bet."

Her eyes narrowed. "Set your terms, Mr. Falcon."

This was getting interesting and could work to my advantage. "If I win, you have to hold off on moving back to Texas and come back on the road with me."

Her gaze roamed over my face as she bit her bottom lip. I knew this look, too. It was her 'weighing every option even though I really want to do it' face, which meant she was considering it.

After a couple long moments, she tilted her head to the side. "Deal. But if I win, you don't get to complain about my job anymore, regardless of what it is."

Hmmm. I was not expecting that curve, but I had faith in myself that I would be the victorious winner in the situation and get my way. After all, I would do anything to keep her with me, even if it meant restraint on my addiction of touching her for one day. In trade I'd get another couple months of her constant companionship on the bus. The longer I kept her on the bus, meant the longer I had to work up the nerve to pop the question of marriage and let her get comfortable with the idea of becoming mine forever.

"You better pack your bags, baby, because you're heading for another extended stay on Big Bertha." I waggled my eyebrows at her.

Lane shook her head. "We'll see," she said in an almost sing-song voice.

"Come here, you," I growled as I pulled her back down for one last round of mind-blowing sex while I was still allowed to touch her.

She squirmed and giggled beneath me as I traced her face with the tip of my index finger. Her green eyes stood out against her olive skin. They were beautiful. It was possible that I might be able to stare into them all day without moving.

Jeesh. What was she doing to me? I was becoming a total pussy.

She swallowed hard and then licked her lips. The mood between us shifted from playful to serious in nearly an instant. The rhythmic pace of her chest increased in speed and I bit my lip as I felt my cock harden against her body.

Even though I couldn't get enough of her body, this crazy chemistry I felt between us stemmed from more than just sex. We had something here.

Love. And it was undeniable.

Every time I thought it wasn't possible to love her anymore, I found my heart swelling more each second I was around her. "I love you so much that sometimes it hurts."

The delicate fingers on her right hand cupped my cheek, and she ran her thumb across my lips. I shut my eyes from the pure exotic pleasure of her intimate touch. Tremors shot down my spine, and my mouth hung open slightly. Lane used that as an invitation to slip her thumb into my mouth a little. I closed my lips around it, tasting her flesh with my tongue.

How was it possible for someone to taste so fucking delicious?

"Noel, I want you," she whispered.

Lane pulled her thumb from my mouth and ran it down the center of my neck, crossing my Adam's apple before she curled her fingers around my neck and pulled my head down. Her lips crashed into mine, and a wave of emotions flooded me. I couldn't be without this. Not for even one damn day. I had to win this bet.

****

Cooking breakfast went relatively smooth. Lane even raised her eyebrows in surprise after I flipped a couple perfect flapjacks onto her waiting plate. Neither of us made a move to touch the other. It was clear that it was game-on at both ends. We were so competitive with each other it was sometimes ridiculous.

We sat across from each other at my small, wooden kitchen table. The late morning sun shined brightly through the windows and lit up every inch of my country-style kitchen. She looked adorable wearing only my t-shirt and her panties with her hair still loose and wild from all the time we spent in my bed earlier.

Lane spread butter across the top of her pancake and drizzled syrup all over as a finishing touch. Just to torture me, she began to lick syrup from each of her fingers in a way that reminded me of a hot porno.

The wheels in my brain turned as I watched her provocatively clean each of her fingers free of the sticky substance. It wasn't hard to picture her pouty lips wrapped around my cock. The mere thought of that caused an ache in my crotch as I felt my dick harden. I have to admit, I would lose my fucking mind if she kept this shit up all damn day. A man can only resist so much temptation.

I gripped the fork in my hand tighter, trying anything to distract me from the thoughts rolling through my head.

Lane smiled and licked her lips. "What's wrong, Noel?"

A rough breath purged from my mouth. "You're kind of evil, you know that?"

She placed her hand on her chest and raised her eyebrows in mock surprise. "Me?"

I rolled my eyes and fought the urge to run around the table and grab her into a huge bear hug for being such a smart-assed tease. "Don't play innocent. You know you're cheating."

She shook her head as she cut into her food with a triumphant smile. "You didn't set any rules in this little game, so how is it that I'm cheating exactly?"

Damn it. She's right. I should've been smarter about setting up this bet. Lane knew I got turned on like a fucking light switch, and she was using that to her advantage.

I leaned back in my chair and stretched out my right leg then quickly pulled it back for fear of accidently touching her with my foot. I clawed at my bare chest out of pure frustration.

Lane snickered after she swallowed a bite of her breakfast.

I shook my head and raked my fingers through my hair. "What I wouldn't give to give you a good spanking right now."

"Well, why don't you?" She licked her lips slowly just to tease me.

A sarcastic laugh tumbled from my mouth. "You'd like that, wouldn't you?"

She cocked her head to the side while her gaze roamed from my face down to my chest. "You have no idea."

Her words nearly sounded like a purr. I tossed my fork on the table, ready to spring into action and give her just what she had requested, then had to steady myself with a few calming breaths. I couldn't take another fucking minute of this. If she kept this shit up, I would most definitely lose and would never be able to finagle another way to get her back on my bus.

I shoved my chair back, leaving my stack of pancakes untouched.

"Where are you going?" Lane cried as I leapt from my chair. "Come back!"

I shook my head. "No way. I'm winning this fucking bet. You fight dirty."

She poked her lip out. "Okay, I'm sorry. I'll play fair. Just come back and eat your breakfast before it gets cold."

My eyes narrowed, but I didn't make a move to sit back down. This made me seem like a pouty little bitch, but there was no way I was going to sit across from her while she continued this torture. If I had to keep my distance for the rest of the day to make that happen, then that was what I was going to do.

Lane crossed her fingers over her heart. "I'll be good. I promise."

I watched her expression sadden for a moment. That look on her face was nearly worse then the seductive one she teased me with only moments ago. Both made me ache to touch her. To hold her in my arms and give her exactly what she needed.

Instead of touching her, I sighed noisily before I plopped back down in my chair.

She smiled. "Thank you. Now eat."

We made it through the rest of our meal without another fight. We talked casually about past friends from high school and what they were up to now. Lane assured me I was definitely the most successful person from our graduating class, while I begged to differ. She was amazing and easily the smartest person I knew.

I cleared my throat. "You know there is one other thing I owe you an apology for."

Lane propped her chin up with her right palm. "What's that?"

"I'm sorry about your job. I know how much it meant to you, and I feel sort of responsible for fucking it up for you."

She shrugged, but her face showed it was still a sore subject. "Diana Swagger is a bitch. Going on the bus with you and her tricking me into that stupid contract just showed me her true colors earlier on. That woman would've never taken me seriously. She told me that to my face. To her I was there for looks. Hell, in her mind I'm sure she would've tried to force me to be your sex slave if it meant getting Black Falcon's marketing rights."

"I detected a sleaze factor from her when I chatted with her on the phone about you, but I still made that deal with her anyway. I guess I was so desperate to get you back, I was willing to make any deal I needed to in order to get you there." Guilt poured over me. Never in my life had I felt as slimy as the day I made that deal with Diana. It was wrong, and I knew it. After Lane walked in on me with the two topless groupies and then the horrible dinner we had, I knew she would never speak to me unless I forced her. My anger when we first reconnected overwhelmed me, and I lashed out at her every chance I could. I was still hurt by her leaving me at the time. I wanted to get back at her, showing her everything she missed out on, and to prove deep down she still wanted me just as much as I wanted her.

Lane stretched her arm across the table and began to reach for my hand. I grinned at how easy winning this bet was about to be, but she pulled her fingers into a tight fist at the last second. "Damn it. I almost forgot."

I raised an eyebrow. "Why don't you go ahead and lose so we can get this over with. You know you want to come back on that bus with me just as much as I need you there."

"Because I'm tired of fighting with you over a stupid job. Winning this bet means you aren't allowed to complain at all, and I like that idea."

It was never her job I didn't like. It was the idea of her using it as an excuse not to give in and finally be with me that pissed me off. I'd admit that it would be hard to allow her to tie herself down to a job in Texas without bitching. If she took a job, she wouldn't be able to just drop everything and join me on tour like I wanted. Being with her all the time was my main goal.

"What?" she asked, shaking me out of my thoughts.

I chewed on the skin on the corner of my thumb. "Nothing, I guess. It's just I was hoping you didn't have to take another job right away. I like the idea of you with me on tour."

She sighed. "Noel, you know I want to be with you too, but I have to find another internship somewhere so I don't throw everything away. I don't really have a choice. I need experience in the marketing field."

"I know, but I don't want to let you go. I just got you back."

Lane stood up and came around the table, stopping at my side. "Let's call truce. You're right. I don't know if I can be away from you either." She held out her hand to me. "At the same time, so we both win. I'll come on the bus with you for a while, if you promise not to bitch whenever I do find another internship or job."

I stared at her hand. This was really the best of both worlds here. One, I could finally touch her again, and two, she'd be on Big Bertha with me. I slid my fingers, which fit perfectly around her tiny hand. Finally having her soft skin against mine sent a tingle up my arm. "Deal."

I slid my chair back and pulled her down into my lap. Her dark hair tickled my nose as I leaned into her and wrapped my arms around her waist. She tossed her arms around my neck and then laid her head on my shoulder. For moments like this with her, I was willing to be anything and everything that she needed, even if that included learning to live apart from her from time to time. Her happiness meant everything to me, and I would try my damndest to always keep a smile on her beautiful face.

Chapter 4

Lane's fingers entwined with mine were what I imagined heaven felt like. Even just that small touch made me feel connected to her. It was nice finally being at peace inside my heart. Waging war on myself over Sophie for the last few months had taken more of a toll on me than I had realized. It made me do crazy, out of my mind things that I would've typically never done.

We continued to walk around my modest property. It wasn't much, but it was the perfect piece of ground. It had vast woods as far as the eye could see set atop high rising hills. There wasn't another soul around for a couple miles, and for some reason that was a totally freeing feeling compared to my typical lifestyle.

After the tour of the empty barn near the house, I lead Lane around the back of the house.

"Where to next, Mr. Tour Guide?" Lane asked.

Michelle A. Valentine

I felt my lips pull into a grin as the dock on my private lake came into view. "My second favorite place in the world."

Lane gasped as she took in the landscape. The hill gradually sloped just like it did at our parent's houses back on Cedar Creek Lake. A slightly overgrown path led down to the entrance of the dock at the bottom. I felt her squeeze my hand a little as the most beautiful smile lit up her face. I knew she would be pleased by this.

"Come on." I gently tugged her forward.

Hand in hand, we made our way down the dirt path in the intense heat of the early summer day. Other than the white railing needing a new coat of paint, everything still seemed in good shape.

Lane slid her hand along the rail once we were on the dock. So many times I dreamt of bringing her out here. There were times I sat out here with my eyes closed and imagined what it used to feel like when I held her in my arms on a dock just like this. For four years, I couldn't shake those thoughts, and now she was here. It was almost surreal, very dream-like.

When we came to the end, I released her hand and wrapped my arm around her shoulders as she leaned on the rail to overlook the water. "Noel, this is perfect. It's almost like being home."

I brushed a loose strand of her hair off her cheek, and she turned her gaze toward me. "This could be home if you wanted it to be."

She twisted her pink lips. "We talked about this, remember? Taking things slow."

"I know, but sometimes it drives me crazy because I already know what I want, and I'm ready to make that happen."

"How can you be so sure?"

"I'm sure because I never want to mess things up with you again. I can't be without you. The only thing that concerns me now is your happiness. I'm just asking for the chance to be your everything. I need to be your forever."

The light stubble on my chin scratched the tips of her fingers when she traced my jaw. "You are my forever, Noel. I promise, no more running."

My heart thundered like a bass drum in my chest. Her green eyes gazed up at me, holding nothing but sincerity to back up her words. For some reason this felt like the perfect moment. What better time to do it but now? We were on a dock. We were fully committed to one another and had voiced we belong to each other forever at different times in the past couple days.

I opened my mouth to pop the question, but the words wouldn't come out. It wasn't that I was afraid or anything. It was the thought of being unprepared. Lane deserved that perfect moment. One like they showed in the movies where the guy surprised her by being totally romantic and thoughtful and presented a ring that meant serious business. I felt unprepared to deliver such a huge moment. I didn't want her to think I was doing this on a whim and wasn't positive this, us, was what I wanted.

My eyes roamed over her face, and I turned her body to face mine. Both of my hands cupped her face. Even though I really wanted to tell her what was on my mind, I panicked and said the first thing that popped in my mind in regards to her last comment. "Good, because chasing you rips my heart out. I want you to stay with me. Always. No more running."

Lane nods. "And no more secrets."

That stung a little. "You're right. No more secrets. From now on, we share everything. No matter if it's something the other probably doesn't want to hear. Deal?"

A slow smile filled her face. "What's with you and all these bets all of the sudden?"

I shrugged. "I like keeping you committed to me, even if it's just a stupid bet."

That was the most ridiculous explanation ever. God! I was becoming a sappy dumb-ass. What the hell was wrong with me?

She lifted one eyebrow and shook her head. "Are you sure you're not crazy?"

I knew it, even Lane thought I was losing it. Who knew trying to figure out how to get the woman I loved to marry me would make me go bat-shit crazy. This situation was getting too heavy.

I took a step back from her and glanced around the quiet lake. Out of the corner of my eye, I saw Lane wipe a little sweat from her brow and it gave me a brilliant idea to lighten up the mood.

"Oh no!" Lane said before she stepped away from me. "Don't even think about it. I know that look."

I kicked off my shoes and laughed. "You might as well lose yours, too, because it's happening."

She made a move to run, but I grabbed her around the waist and then hoisted her over my shoulder. Both of her feet kicked wildly as I attempted to remove her shoes. When she didn't hold still, I gave her ass a smack just hard enough to sting through her cut-off shorts.

Her shriek echoed around the open water as I yanked her shoes off one by one. "Noel, I swear, don't throw me in that water!"

I carried her to the edge of the dock. "One."

"Noel..." she warned.

"Two."

"No. Wait!"

"Three!" I laughed and tossed Lane into the clear water of the lake.

The water rippled around the spot she went under, and when her head popped above water a couple seconds later, I dove in beside her still fully clothed. The crisp water shocked my summer-heated body to the core, and for an instant I felt a little evil for throwing her in here, but forgave myself a second later after I adjusted and it felt like heaven.

She splashed water in my face. "You asshole! I still have all my clothes on."

My pierced eyebrow quirked up on its own accord. "Like I've told you before, clothing is optional around me. I prefer you naked."

I reached through the water until my hands found her torso so I could yank her against my body. Even through the chilled water, I could feel my temperature rise. She just had that effect on me. My eyes peered down at her chest as the thought of Lane in a wet t-shirt crossed my mind.

Michelle A. Valentine

"What's that smirk all about?" she teased.

I bit my lip. "Just how fucking hot you'll look when we get out of this water in that white tank-top." I reached over and traced her bra strap with my fingertips. "If only you weren't wearing this."

Her smile turned wicked as she turned away from me while treading water. With some crazy-mad skill, she pulled her shirt up just high enough to reveal her bra hook and reached behind her and did a one handed flip to unclasp it. She faced me again once her shirt was down so that I could witness her masterfully removed her bra without taking off her shirt. It swirled around the air a few times in her hand before she chucked it up on the dock.

"That was impressive," I laughed, fully enjoying her slight strip tease.

Lane threw her arms around my neck and leaned in and pressed her soft lips against mine. I would never get enough of her sweet taste. I plunged my tongue into her mouth and wished I could bury other parts of my body inside her.

It was difficult to get the closeness I craved while treading water, so I knew I needed to end this before I got so turned on I tried to fuck her right here in the lake. Sex in water was never my preference. I much preferred to slide into a woman with ease caused by her natural arousal.

I pushed away from Lane and grinned before I quickly placed my hand on top of her head and shoved her under for a mood shift. The thought alone of being inside Lane was enough to make my dick hard.

She resurfaced, fighting mad. "You're such an asshole!"

I laughed as she splashed water in my face again. "So you keep telling me, but I know that's just another way of you saying you love me."

She rolled her eyes, and I knew I was right.

Chapter 5

I rolled over in the darkness and stretched my arm over a cold spot in the bed where Lane's body should be. I sat up and looked around, still half asleep. There were no lights on around me, and I felt panic rip through me. I sat up and called out her name, but didn't receive an answer.

There wasn't any noise as my bare feet padded across the wooded floor towards the master bathroom. "Lane?" I tried again—still no answer.

I crept down the dark hall and flicked on the light and headed down the stairs. When I got into the great room, I froze at the sight of Lane curled up under a blanket on the leather sofa. Panic washed through me as the reasons she wasn't sleeping in bed with me popped into my brain.

Just as I opened my mouth to wake her and ask what she was doing, she erupted into a coughing fit. Oh no. She was sick.

I tiptoed over to her and placed my hand on her forehead. "You're burning up," I said it more to myself then anything.

Leaving her fast asleep, I went into the bathroom to find a thermometer and ibuprofen. I rummaged through my medicine cabinet, slinging bottles out of the way until I found the pain reliever, but no thermometer. After cursing myself for not being better prepared for a situation like this, I went to the kitchen to retrieve a glass of water for Lane.

I returned to find her scrunched into a ball and shivering. I almost felt guilty for waking her, but I knew she needed medicine for the fever. "Lane?" I nudged her arm. "Lane, wake up. I brought you some medicine."

She groaned and then opened her eyes. "I didn't wake you, did I?"

I shook my head—silly girl. "No. I was just worried when you weren't in bed, so I came to find you. Here." I held out the glass for her. "This is ibuprofen."

Both of her arms shook a little as she pushed her weight up off the couch and then took the glass and pills from me. "I don't know what's happened to me. I felt fine when we went to bed."

A frown pulled on my lips as the thought crossed my mind that somehow I made her sick by throwing her in the water earlier today. My fingers raked through my hair.

"Don't do that," she said.

I stopped and tilted my head. "What?"

She swallowed the pills and chased it down with a gulp of water. "Blame yourself for this. I'm sick. It happens. I'm sure the virus was in my system long before you tried to drown me today."

Her mind reading ability was uncanny. Sometimes it was easy to forget she knew me just as well as I knew her. "I'm calling a doctor in town first thing in the morning."

Lane closed her eyes and shook her head. "No. I don't want to go anywhere. Just let me sleep this off."

"You won't have to go anywhere. I've have him come here."

Her fingers trembled as she rubbed her forehead. "Doctors don't make house calls anymore, Noel."

The look on her face told me she was in pain. Quickly, I readjusted the pillows. "Lay back down. You don't look so good."

Once I had her in a comfortable position, I went to the hall closet and grabbed another blanket for myself. I dimmed the lights from the stairway, and then made my way over to the over-sized recliner next to the couch.

"What are you doing?" she asked as I plopped down and then kicked my feet out.

"Getting comfortable, so I can try to get some sleep."

"You don't have to suffer along with me."

I raised an eyebrow at her ridiculous statement. "Where you go, I go. If you are in misery, then I'm going to be there to help you. Now, get some rest."

****

Lane wasn't any better in the morning, so I called the local physician's office and rolled my eyes when I heard one of the women in the office actually squeal when the receptionist told her who was on the phone. The squealer got on the phone and asked how she could help me. She had that nervous little giggle in her voice that some women get when they talk to me. I tried to be as polite as possible without getting annoyed.

"Well, Ma'am—"

"Tammy," she corrected while cutting me off with another giggle.

I sighed. "Tammy, my girlfriend is sick and I need Dr. Malone to come to my place and see her."

"Oh, my goodness, I'm sorry Mr. Falcon, but Dr. Malone doesn't do home visits. Can't you just bring her in?"

I pinched the bridge of my nose. "Can you please just check with him? When I moved here, the mayor told me because of my…status he would have Dr. Malone make an exception for me."

"I don't know who—"

This chick was going to be tough to crack. A little charm might go a long way with this one. "Tammy, sweetheart, I know you're just doing your job, but it would be a huge favor to me personally if you could just check with him or even let me speak with him. I will pay him cash. Please?"

There was silence for a moment, but then she said, "All right. Let me put you on hold."

I did a fist pump. Being a celebrity sometimes had its perks. "Thank you."

Tammy returned to the line and asked, "What's the address? He can come out during his lunch hour."

I rattled off my address and thanked her profusely before I hung up. For a fleeting second it crossed my mind that all the women in that office now had my personal information, and I hoped they didn't plan a visit themselves.

Back in the living room, Lane's face was pale, and dark circles had formed under her eyes as she watched television.

"Hey," I greeted her as I sat down next to her. "How you feeling?"

"Lousy." She attempted to scoot away from me, but I grabbed her around the waist and slid her back to me. "What are you doing? I can't get you sick."

"I don't care about that."

She snuggled into my side. "You may not, but your fans will if you can't make your shows."

"You're more important then my shows." And I meant that. She was my everything. "Dr. Malone will be here around lunch time to check you out."

"I guess you do have some pull after all."

I rubbed her arm and kissed her blazing-hot forehead. "I don't know why you continue to doubt my mad skills."

A chuckle turned into a slight cough as she leaned away and reached for the toilet paper roll I had brought her in lieu of tissues. The cough was starting to sound worse, too. I hoped this doctor hurried up.

After my attempt to get Lane to eat some chicken noodle soup failed, there was a knock on the door. Relief flooded me as I knew this man could help her in way I couldn't.

Rock the Band

On the other side of my door stood a stout little guy, who couldn't be much taller than five foot. His red hair was thin on top, but still thick on the sides, while his neatly trimmed beard perfectly matched the color of his hair. He kind of reminded me of one of those munchkins from the *Wizard of Oz*, just a slight bit thinner.

"Dr. Malone?" I questioned since he didn't have a white coat on or anything, merely a pair of khaki pants and a cheap looking button down shirt.

The man pushed by me and walked into the living room without a word. If he wasn't my only chance at getting Lane better, I would've tossed him back out the door on his ass for being such a pompous dick.

His beady eyes shifted onto Lane who sat shaking on the sofa under a blanket. "You the sick girl?"

Lane nodded and licked her dry lips. "Yesss, sir."

For being such a little man, he seemed like he could intimidate the shit out of people when he wanted.

"Fever?"

Lane shrugged. "We don't have a thermometer, but I think so."

The doctor narrowed his eyes at me. "What kind of person doesn't keep a thermometer on hand?"

I flinched at his snippy tone. People didn't usually speak to me that way. "The kind of person who is very busy."

He laughed, but it was thick with sarcasm. "Son, don't tell me about being busy. I'm busy from the time I get up, until the time I go to bed seeing patients. Even making house calls to our new resident celebrities because they feel too prestigious to come down to my clinic, yet I guarantee you I have one at my house."

My jaw ached as I ground my teeth together to keep me from lashing out. Instead I took a deep breath. "I guess I'm slacking then."

Satisfied with my answer, he sat the small black bag he carried in with him on the coffee table and opened it. He produced the thermometer and cleaned it with an alcohol wipe before placing it under Lane's arm. Dr. Malone also pulled a stethoscope and went to work listening to Lane's lungs. A couple seconds later the thermometer beeped, and I attempted to read it over his shoulder before he blocked my view.

"Young lady, your axillary temperature is one hundred point three. That accompanied with the cough and the wheezing and crackles I hear in your lungs tells me you've got a nasty infection. I'm going to go ahead and give you some samples of an antibiotic that the pharmaceutical company has graciously supplied my office with for patients. Also here's a decongestant."

He pulled two white bottles from his bag and hands them to Lane. "Use the liquid medication every four hours as needed for cough, and take one pill every twelve hours until they're all gone, regardless if you feel better. Understand?"

She nodded and he closed his bag. "Good. Now, there's a matter of payment to discuss."

Dr. Malone turned towards me expectantly. Right. Money. I walked into the kitchen and grabbed the cookie jar from the overhead cabinet above the stainless steel refrigerator. Not the most original place to keep a wad of cash, but it worked.

I counted out five hundred dollars, not really sure what a physician's time was worth, and handed to the little man on the other side of my counter. "Will this cover it?"

He took the money from my hand and recounted it right in front of me. "It'll do. Call the office if you need anything else."

And just as quickly as the doctor had wafted into my home, he found his way back out.

I watched through the window as he shut himself inside his car and then sped back down the drive.

"He was an odd one, wasn't he?" Lane's voice caught my attention and I immediately went into the kitchen to retrieve something for her to drink so she could take her new medications.

I handed her the glass. "Yeah, not much of a bedside manner."

"Right? That was exactly what I was thinking," she said before swallowing down the meds.

It was good to see a smile on her face even though I knew she still felt miserable. I sat down and then pulled her head down so she could rest it in my lap. My fingers stroked through her soft hair. We settled in together watching some movie on television but it wasn't long before we both were fast asleep.

Chapter 6

After a couple days of tender love and care from me, Lane was starting to come back around. It was a good thing we came to my place when we did. Being sick on the bus is the closest thing to hell I've ever experienced, so I was happy she didn't have to suffer through that.

The oven timer chimed, and I removed our extra crispy tater-tots. I really needed to go to the store. Living off frozen food was starting to suck.

"Something smells good," Lane said as she dried her hair with a green towel, wearing only one of my t-shirts.

I smiled. I loved it when she wore my clothes. "You feel like eating?"

She draped the towel along the back of the kitchen chair and gave me a wicked grin. "I'm really hungry. I've been a little deprived lately."

I swallowed hard and licked my lips. We'd gone without sex for a couple days now, and the way her eyes raked over my body when she'd slowly said the word hungry told me she'd been missing it, too.

After a couple steps toward her, I tugged her body into mine. Both of her arms wrapped snuggly against my waist. The smell of her fruity scents from the shower still surrounded her. Instantly my breathing picked up.

I raised an eyebrow. "Feeling better?"

She traced a line from my chest down to my belt buckle. "Much."

With sure fingers she unzipped my jeans and snaked her hand inside. She grabbed my hard dick and a smirk played on her lips. "I'm so buying you underwear for Christmas."

I laughed. "Don't count on me wearing them."

When I leaned down to kiss her lips, she jerked her head back, and a frown filled my face. "Let me kiss you."

Her brow crinkled a bit. "Noel, you can't."

"Don't worry about that, Lane. Like I said, I don't care if I get sick."

"But I do. Can't we just get creative?" Her finger traced my jaw.

My heart thudded against my ribs at what the word *creative* meant. This could be fun. "What do you have in mind?"

"We shouldn't be face to face."

Oh dear God. She was asking me to bend her over and take her from behind. My cock pulsed and it was nearly painful how much it ached to be inside her. She wrapped her hand around me and stroked me a couple times while she waited on me to respond. I closed my eyes, enjoying her touch, and allowed my mouth to hang open a bit. Both of my hands tightly gripped the hem of her shirt. Simple touches from his girl drove me crazy.

I wrapped my hand around her wrist, stopping her motion. I needed to slow things down before I exploded all over the inside of my pants.

Lane took the hint and shoved my pants down to my knees. "I want you inside me."

Every cell vibrated with need. Without thinking about it, I pushed her shirt up and yanked on her bra, ripping it from her body. I tugged on each side of her panties until they dropped by her feet. I couldn't get her naked fast enough.

She kicked them off, and I lifted her onto the counter. I dropped to my knees and placed soft kisses from her ankle to her exposed thigh. Both of her legs fell open for me and she watched me intently. I slid her ass to the edge of the counter and threw her left leg over my shoulder before I licked my way down to her moist heat. The scent of her arousal was nearly enough to make me want to come on the spot. I loved how ready she always was for me.

I took my time licking each of her folds before giving her clit the attention I knew she craved. She whimpered every time I got close, which told me I was doing my job. I knew the anticipation of getting off drove her mad, but I also knew how much better it made the final moment of release when it had to be worked for.

My tongue darted out and drew the figure eight around her sweet spot. Fingers grabbed my hair and urged me in deeper. A quick peek at her face told me she was close. Her eyes were squeezed shut, and she propped herself up with one hand while she plucked her nipple with the other.

I circled her opening before ramming a finger inside her.

"God, Noel!" she screamed and locked her ankles behind my head.

She needed off badly. I sucked her clit in my mouth, tasting all of her in the process, then flicked it with my tongue as fast as I could.

She sucked in a quick breath and groaned as she came hard against my lips while her walls clenched greedily at my finger. She let my head go but still writhed with need before me.

I stood up and picked her up from the counter, anxious to be inside her.

"Turn around," I ordered roughly in her ear, desperately needing release of my own.

The soft skin of her back pressed against my chest, and it took everything in me not to ram my cock deep inside her ready core. I whipped her shirt over her head and tossed it to the ground. I rubbed my hand across her back and then into her hair and finally pushed down until her elbows rested on the counter in front of her. I knelt in behind her and hiked her leg up so I could lap at her wet folds again. She pushed back against my tongue, eager for more.

She was so ready for me.

I rose up and grabbed the base of my shaft and rubbed it in her juices before guiding it inside her.

"Fuck!" It came out almost like a growl. It just felt so good, and I couldn't stop myself from voicing just how amazing she felt finally wrapped around me.

I gripped her right hip with one hand and her left shoulder with the other as I worked in and out of her a few more times. Soon after she was good and ready I drove deep into her.

The noises that came from her mouth sent a wave of pleasure through me. I loved when she enjoyed something sexually as much as I did.

As I nearly was ready to lose my mind, I laid my chest on her back as I reached around her hips with my right hand. I fingered her sweet spot. "Come with me."

"You like it when I do that?" Lane said, her voice full of passion.

Oh my God. "You have no idea how much I fucking love it."

"Then fuck me harder." My eyes widened with those dirty words coming from those sweet lips.

I bit my lip as I pounded into her full force.

"Oh, God!" she screamed as she gripped the counter.

"Ah!" It was all I could get out before my hot seed spurted inside her tight little body.

I lay gasping as I wrapped my arms around her waist. Every time with this woman was better than the last. We connected on so many levels it was crazy. She was truly my soul mate.

Chapter 7

The rest of the week flew by too damn fast, and Tuesday morning came before I was ready.

Kyle pulled up in the Escalade and honked the horn. I was thankful Lane was nearly better now that we were going back on the bus.

I carried our luggage outside and stacked it on the porch so Kyle could load it. "Hey, man. Find your way back all right."

Kyle nodded and tucked his hair behind his ears. "Yeah, it wasn't too bad."

Lane came up beside me, and I wrapped my arm around her shoulders. "I can't believe we have to go back already."

I sighed. "Tell me about it. I never get enough time off. Sometimes I feel like running away for a while."

She leaned her head against me. "That's a nice dream, but I think your legion of fangirls would track you down if you stayed hidden for too long."

"If they're hot, I wouldn't mind so much," I teased and she smacked my ass. "Ouch!"

She raised an eyebrow and shot me look that revealed she didn't think my little joke was too funny.

I threaded our fingers together. "Come on. Let's head back to civilization."

About twenty minutes into our drive and hearing all about Kyle's week with his girl Emily, Lane's cell chirped. She dug into her purse and fished out her phone. "We finally have service."

Even though I knew it wasn't polite or good boyfriend etiquette to peek at her phone, I glanced down at the screen. Ten missed calls flashed before she dialed in the code to listen to her messages.

A distinctly male voice was on the line, and my ears perked up.

Lane twisted her lips as she listened and then after a couple seconds grinned. Why was she smiling? I was trying not to be a jealous dick, but I didn't like it when another man made her face light up like that. That was my fucking job.

She hung up the phone and stared at me. "That was Striker."

Both of my hands curled into fists on my lap. "What did he want?"

"To offer me a job," she said. "Isn't that great news?"

I shook my head. "No."

"No? What do you mean, no? This is a great opportunity."

How could she not see what he was doing? This job wasn't a goodwill gesture. It was a way to keep her close. That asshole obviously still didn't get it. Lane was mine and he needed to move the fuck on and quit trying to go after my girl. It wasn't going to happen for him. "You can't work for him."

Lane's eyebrows furrowed. "You promised you wouldn't complain about any job I took. I can't believe you're acting like this. I know this isn't the ideal situation or boss, but there's nothing between Striker and me."

A sarcastic laugh slipped from me. "Maybe on your end."

"Noel…don't be that way. I need this job."

I grabbed her hand. "But you don't need this job. I'll take care of you."

She pulled her hand away. "I don't want to be taken care of. Don't you understand? I need a life outside of us—independence. The job Striker's offering allows me to remain on tour with you and still work. He won't be around like you think. It's the best of both worlds."

I folded my arms across my chest and attempted to listen calmly. "What kind of job?"

She grinned. "It's putting together an online marketing campaign for a new line of men's jewelry Striker has designed with a jeweler. It's a personal project for him."

I raised my pierced eyebrow. "Men's jewelry? I knew that British fucker was part fairy."

Lane laughed and smacked my leg. "Be nice."

I held up my hands defensively. "What? Just stating the obvious."

She rolled her eyes at me, and I tugged her body against mine in the seat. "This is serious, Noel."

I sighed. "I know. I'm sorry, but you have to admit he's a tool."

"He's pretty nice to me."

"Yeah, because he wants in your panties. But I've got news for him. It isn't happening. Those panties belong to me."

She gave me a pointed look. "Do they?"

I leaned down and kissed her lips before I worked my way to her ear. "We both know you love screaming my name when you come. So yeah, they belong to me," I growled.

Lane blushed fiercely. I knew that was fighting dirty, but when it came to claiming her, there were no rules. She was mine, and I wasn't above reminding her or anyone else of that from time to time.

We pulled into the parking lot a little later, and Big Bertha was a comforting sight with the regular crew gathered around it. Although I didn't know the roadies all too well, it was good to see their familiar faces.

Kyle parked the SUV near the back of the bus and hopped out.

"Feel good to be back?" Lane asked as I helped her out.

"Yes and no. I miss the guys, but there's never enough alone time with you."

She threw her arms around my neck. "See, then you should be happy about this job."

My shoulders tensed under her touch. "I'm just not happy about your new boss."

She traced my chin with her finger. "Nothing will happen between me and Striker. I love *you*. So quit worrying."

It was easy to trust Lane, but it was hard to trust that douchebag, Striker. Who knew what his plan was. Everything inside of me told me it wasn't just to give Lane a job. She was a beautiful woman. Any man would've told you that, and that's why it didn't add up.

"I could always try to get the Black Falcon account back from Center Stage," I told her, hoping it changed her mind.

She shook her head. "No. They have Aubrey working on it now, and I can't take that away from her."

I knew Aubrey was her best friend and she and Riff kind of had a thing, but her career wasn't what mattered to me. I guess I was just a selfish jerk because taking something away from Aubrey to give to Lane was something I would've tried in a heartbeat if she wanted it. But she would kill me if I did that. There didn't seem to be a way around her taking this new job.

I sighed again and felt utterly defeated. "You won't be around him much?"

"If ever," she countered.

"If it makes you happy, then I'll try my best to be supportive."

Her lips crushed into mine. "And that is why you're the best boyfriend in the entire world."

I grinned and ground my pelvis into hers. "I thought this made me the best."

She smacked my chest. "You are impossible."

I laughed. "But you love me."

The skin on her cheeks was so soft as I cradled her face in my hands. I dipped my head and planted my lips on hers.

"Oh, God! Would you two get a room already?" a voice remarked behind us. "A week of fuck time didn't get it out of your systems?"

I turned to find Trip grinning like an idiot. "Don't be a jealous asshole. Someday you'll find a woman you don't have to pay."

"Ha. Ha. Very funny, dickhead. Now come on and get your asses on the bus. We've been waiting for twenty minutes on you two so we could head out."

I nodded to him. "All right. We're coming. Simmer down, saucy."

He flipped me off and headed for the bus. I turned back to Lane. "Come on, before he gets his panties in a bunch."

Once inside, it was good to see nothing had changed. All the guys were present and accounted for. Tyke and Trip busied themselves with restocking the kitchen with supplies, while Riff talked on his cell with a stack of Oreos in front of him. With my girl at my side, all things were right with the world. Everyone that mattered, with the exception of my mom, was here on this bus.

Lane kissed my cheek, and I watched her with a huge smile on my face head towards the bedroom to settle in.

Tyke handed me a beer from across the island. "Good break? I see that sappy grin."

I twisted off the cap. "Don't hate."

Tyke held his hands up palms up. "I'm not. It's just going to be weird around here with both you and Riff settled down and all."

The liquid in my mouth nearly strangled me. "Riff?" I peered over at my friend sitting at the table wearing a goofy grin while he talked quietly on the phone. "With who?"

Tyke gave me a pointed look. "Lane's friend, Aubrey. Who else?"

My eyebrows rose. "Realllllly? Wow. I thought they just hooked up."

He shrugged. "Apparently he spent the entire break with her in New York, and he's been on the phone with her now for the last hour."

"Huh." I was shocked. My best friend was a totally the bag 'em and leave 'em type. The only person he'd ever had a long-term relationship with was Sophie, and even that had only lasted two months before she claimed to have slept with me, but he never acted like he was smitten with her. There must've been something about Aubrey that hooked him. For as long as I had known him, I'd never seen that happen before.

Tyke chugged the rest of his beer and then tossed it in the trash. "Did you hear Attack Jacket dropped off the rest of the tour?"

"What? When did this happen and why am I just now hearing about this?"

"Try getting a landline out in that no man's land you live in. We couldn't get a hold of you."

"Well who did the label get to cover?"

Tyke cocked his head. "Who does the label always get to cover?"

Fuck me. Shit. Shit. Shit. Not that asshole. Now his little scheme to get Lane to work for him was starting to make sense. He knew he was going to be around her and planned on using it for an excuse.

Damn his sneaky ass.

This was so not good. Striker needed to know Lane was off limits. If I slapped a huge carat of commitment on her finger, he sure as hell would take the hint to back the fuck off.

The perfect proposal was just going to have to be skipped. When I got a minute away, I was going to buy a ring and ask her the first chance I got.

Chapter 8

The next night Lane and I were backstage while Embrace the Darkness wrapped up their set. I never had a problem with them opening for us before, not until their frontman, Striker, tried to put the moves on my girl. Now, it was eating me alive I was so agitated by it.

The crowd loved them, screaming and interacting with the band. Women seemed to go crazy for the long-haired British front man. He got nearly as may panties tossed at him as Riff and I.

"Goodnight, Nashville!" Striker screamed over the microphone before he waved and exited the stage towards us.

The moment his eyes locked on Lane, a grin broke out of his face. "Lane, it's good to see you. I'm excited to see what that marketing brain of yours comes up with for the line."

"Thank you for the opportunity. It'll look great on my resume," Lane answered.

"No problem, love." He smiled at her.

My jaw muscle clenched. I hated when he called her that and didn't care if it was part of his British slang. It seemed too personal. And that smile. I was ready to knock it off his face.

As if on cue, Lane's cell phone rang with her special "Your mother's calling" ringtone. "I'm sorry. I have to take this."

She stepped away from to take the call privately. I watched Striker's eyes follow her, and I felt my blood boil beneath my skin. "I'm on to you."

He snapped his gaze back to me and smirked. "Oh, yeah? Better be on your bloody toes then, mate."

My eyes narrowed, and I closed the gap between us. "Watch it, fucker. I didn't get to finish the job last time."

Striker tipped his head up and stared at me. "It wasn't quite a fair fight last time. Let's see you try it when my back isn't turned."

Air rushed through my nostrils as I took a huge breath. Adrenaline flowed through my veins. This guy needed ended.

"Hey!" Lane's voice rang in my ears as she shoved between us. "What's going on here?"

Striker stepped back. "Ask your boyfriend," he said before turning and walking away. "Lane, we'll be in touch."

She furrowed her brow at me the moment Striker was out of earshot. "What the hell, Noel? You promised."

She started to storm away, but I caught her arm. "Wait, Lane. I'm sorry, but the things he was saying—"

"Don't mean a thing! Regardless of *his* intentions, you need to trust *me*. Have faith in my love for you."

My heart pounded in my chest as I dropped her arm and allowed her to walk away. She was right. Relationships were built on trust, and I sure as hell didn't want to crumble mine by being an overbearing control freak.

I ran my fingers through my hair as I watched her leave.

"Ten minutes, Mr. Falcon," the stage manager said as he walked by me.

"Okay. Yeah," I answered numbly as a thousand thoughts of how I nearly just screwed over my relationship with Lane went through my mind.

It was hard for me to focus my entire set. On our fourth song, I screwed up the lyrics. Riff's gaze whipped in my direction, and he crinkled his brow. Fighting with Lane always fucked with my head. I needed to get my shit together.

The crowd roared as I belted out the chorus of the last song. Sweat dripped down my face and back as I ran to each side of the stage and hyped them up. Their fists pumped in the air to the beat pounded out by Trip. The stage lights beamed down on me as I gripped the mic and sang one last note of *Ball Busting Bitch*, our biggest hit so far.

The drums got a few more kicks and then silence took over. "Thank you, Nashville!"

I wiped my face with a white towel and tossed it into the crowd. It landed about fifteen feet into the crowd and instantly the shoving began. It always puzzled me why people would fight over a towel covered in my sweat.

Riff threw his arm around my neck as I walked off stage. "What's up, buddy? Want to talk about it?"

Sometimes I hated how he knew when shit was on my mind. Riff had always been the guy in the band I went to when things were on my mind, and I could tell him anything. But it was hard to admit hard to admit to him that I was still having woman problems. I was sure he was sick of hearing this from me by now.

Finally I shook my head. "Nah, man it's cool. Just a little off tonight, you know."

He dropped his arm from around my shoulders. "Okay, but if you need to talk, you know where to find me."

"Thanks, but really, I'm cool." There was no need to drag him into this mess.

Once he was convinced I was good, he took off. Normally I would've said he was off to find his random groupie for the night, but from what I'd heard, Riff seemed to be really into Aubrey and I wondered if he would find a girl for the night. I guess we'd see just how serious he was about Lane's friend.

After I fought my way through the fans, I advised Kyle to take a break for the rest of the evening. I needed to talk things over with Lane, preferably alone.

The bus was quiet. The rest of the guys were still out living down the high of being on stage. Sometimes it was tough to work off all of that adrenaline without blowing off a little steam. My go-to relief used to be the arms of random women. But those days were nothing but a distant memory, ones I would love to forget.

"Lane?" I called down the hall. "Are you in here?"

When she didn't answer, I panicked. Where could she be? Even though I hated myself for thinking it, the first place or person she might've been with was Striker. She just yelled at me for not trusting her, and here I was letting crazy images of my worst fear cloud my better judgment.

The foxholes were empty. So far, I didn't see another soul on this bus.

The bedroom door was partially closed. With a slightly shaky hand, I pushed it open. There was no sign of her. The bed was still perfectly made, and our luggage was still zipped up tight.

I sighed and rubbed the back of my neck. When was I ever going to stop fucking up with this girl?

Behind me, the bus door closed with a thud. I whirled around, and my gaze landed on Lane. Her green eyes were puffy, like she'd been crying since the last moment I had seen her. Without thinking about it, I made a beeline for her. I wrapped my arms around her tiny waist and buried my face in her dark curls. She sobbed as she threw her arms around my neck and held onto me just as hard as I held on to her.

"I'm so sorry, Lane. I trust you—I do—but Striker just gets under my skin. The things he was insinuating about you… It's him I don't trust, but I need to learn to trust that you'd knee him square in the balls if he tried shit with you."

She laughed at my lame attempt to be funny while I apologized. "I'm sorry too. I should always have your side, and I'm sorry I didn't give you a chance to explain yourself. I won't take the job if bothers you that much."

I pulled back and cupped her face. "No. Take the job. I'll try harder to be understanding and trust your judgment."

"Thank you," she whispered before I kissed her lips and proceeded to finish making it up to her.

Chapter 9

After Lane had gone to bed, I had spent the better part of the night searching engagement rings. There were tons of really fancy rings, but for some reason, the simplistic styles spoke to me the most. They were the ones that practically screamed Lane at me. I wanted a very classic two-carat diamond ring set in white gold

First thing in morning, I called the local jeweler and told him exactly what I wanted, and they assured me they could hook me up. After that, I texted Kyle and told him I would need his help distracting Lane. When he asked why, I answered with the truth. If anyone would understand what it was like to really be in love with someone, it was Kyle.

After he agreed, Lane and I headed out with him for a little shopping. She wanted a new pair of sandals, and I had my mission to somehow covertly buy the ring. Sales people were always eager to please.

"It's nice to feel normal for a change," Lane said while she sat next to me in the back of the Escalade.

Kyle laughed from the front. "You mean getting chased by hoards of screaming women isn't normal? After only being here a few weeks, I was starting to believe that was the norm."

"Hang around Black Falcon long enough, and it definitely does become an everyday occurrence," she teased.

I rolled my eyes. As much as I didn't like it, there was truth in their words. It was very difficult to feel normal and not allow the day in and day out fame to rush to my head. When the band took off, I almost felt invincible, like no one could touch me or hurt me. I was on top of the world, and everybody wanted me.

Well, not the people I really wanted to want me like Lane and my own father.

My head slunk against the seat. Every time my thoughts focused on my father my spirits always came down. Why didn't he love me? Was having a dream so wrong that you wished your only son had never been born?

Well according to my asshole father, the answer was yes.

The night Lane dumped my ass out on the dock, I was a wreck. I destroyed my room and smashed my guitar. All of it meant nothing without her. She was my world, even back then, and without her, it was a very dark place. Dad had no sympathy for me. In fact, he even voiced how smart Lane had been to get rid of a loser like me before I ruined her life.

That hurt, but the crushing blow came when he said he regretted having me at all. To hear my own parent express pure hatred for me was something I would never forget. Lane had broached the subject of making up with my father for my mother's sake, but I just couldn't bring myself to do it.

What did I have to apologize for?

"Hey. You okay?" Lane asked her face etched with concern.

"I'm fine, just tired," I lied.

I didn't want Lane or anybody to know how much not having a relationship with my father bothered me. It was better for people to think I hated him versus being the sad, pathetic sap not even a parent could love.

Kyle parked along the street, just in between the jewelry store and the shoe store. It was nearly the perfect set up. Now the trick was going to be getting in and out of there without Lane getting suspicious or figuring out what I was doing. She hated when I did things that she thought pushed our relationship too fast. She'd kill me if she knew what I was up to already.

Having this ring would show her I meant business.

"This is perfect, Kyle. Thanks," I said.

He flicked his gaze to the review mirror, and he nodded, understanding my secret code.

I helped Lane out of the SUV, and as if on cue, my cell rang. I peered down at the caller I.D. and frowned. "I have to take this. You guys go on in. I'll be there in a minute."

I kissed Lane's cheek as Kyle led her into the shoe store. As soon as Lane turned her back I swiped my thumb over the end call button and pressed the phone to my ear. It really was a touch of pure genius when I arranged Kyle to call my cell just outside the store. A phone call was a believable diversion to distract Lane long enough without getting her suspicions up.

Less than thirty seconds later, I stepped inside. The privately owned store was small, but there were amazing looking pieces inside the glass show cases. Each diamond seemed to outshine the next as I made my way down the counter to greet the white haired salesman at the end.

"Hi." I cleared my throat. All of the sudden my stomach clenched, and I felt a slight tingle of excitement inside my chest. This was it—the next to last step in getting Lane to agree to marry me.

"Yeah, hi," I tried again. "I called earlier about holding a ring for me."

The older man's eyes lit up, and his smiled caused deep crinkle lines around his eyes to form. "Ah, yes, Mr. Falcon. I have that piece right here for you."

He unlocked the safe behind him with a key that was attached to a bracelet he wore around his wrist. He removed a ring set in a tiny black velvet box and placed it on the glass counter in front of me. As promised, it was the exact ring I had picked out online. The single diamond gleamed against the lights in the shop, and my heart squeezed almost painfully. It was one of the most beautiful things I'd ever seen. Not so much the ring itself, but what it stood for.

Instantly, I saw Lane's face in my mind. What it would look like when she saw it. The way her mouth would move when she said the one tiny word I longed to hear when I gave it to her. *Yes.*

This was the ring. It was like it was made just for her, and I wanted to be the man who gave it to her.

"I'll take it," I told the man as I ripped my wallet from my back pocket.

He nodded curtly and eagerly took the card from my hand and swiped it nearly immediately, before returning with the card and slip for me to sign.

My sloppy signature graced the receipt for ten thousand dollars. Granted it wasn't the typical million dollar ring most stars bought when they got married, but Lane and I weren't like everyone else. We were just us, plain and simple, a lot like the ring itself.

"Thank you for your business, Mr. Falcon. I wish the best to you and your love," the man said as he attempted to place the ring box and paperwork in a bag.

I shook my head. "No bag or paperwork needed."

The old man shrugged as I slipped the ring box safely into my front pocket before making my way out of the store.

Twenty minutes later, Lane had picked two new pairs of shoes, and we were on our way back to Big Bertha. We were scheduled to leave for the next city on the tour, which I believed was Atlanta, in about an hour. Proposing on the bus wasn't ideal, neither was in the back of this vehicle with Kyle right up front, but this ring was burning a hole in my pocket. Plus, I couldn't wait to see it on her finger.

I took her left hand into both of mine as she stared off over my right shoulder at the passing building. A cold sweat broke out all over my body. What the hell was wrong with me? I could sing in front of thousands of people without so much as a second thought, but was freaking out over asking my best friend and long-time love to marry me.

Get it together, Noel!

Lane turned towards me and glanced down at my hands clinging to her. "You okay?"

I nodded a little too enthusiastically. "Yeah. Yeah, I'm great."

An uneasy laugh came out of her as she studied me intently.

Shit. My mind was blank. Writing songs about love and loss with her in mind, even with dyslexia, came easy, but phrasing something amazing that would blow her away on the spot was kicking my ass. No words came to mind to describe just how much she meant to me.

She opened her mouth then quickly closed it before digging her phone from her pocket. Her mother's signature ringtone filled the air.

"Sorry," she apologized to me before answering her phone. "Hi, Mom."

Never had I been so glad for a couple minute reprieve in order to get my nerves together and pound this muddled mess in my brain down into something that made sense.

"What?" Lane's voice kicked up a couple octaves, and she flinched. "What do you mean broke your leg? Oh my God, Mom! Are you okay?"

I held her hand tighter, but not for the same reason as before. Now, I was worried. Kathy was like a second mother to me, and I was concerned for her well-being.

"Okay, I'm coming down there. As soon as I get back to the bus, I'll get packed and book a flight."

Shit. I settled back in the seat. This wasn't the time to give her the ring. It was best if I waited a couple days until she came back from helping out her mom.

A couple minutes later we parked next to the bus, and Lane ended her call. "So, Mom took a nasty fall while trying to clear a bird's nest from the gutter on her house. She broke her right leg in two places and needs surgery."

"That's terrible. Is there anything I can do to help?"

"No, but I will have to go help her for a while. Hopefully, Striker will understand that I won't be around to consult, and he'll be okay with working with me via email until Mom's back on her feet."

I knitted my brow in confusion. I didn't like the sound of this. "How long will you be gone?"

Lane frowned, and my stomach dropped. That was the face she got when she was about to tell me something I didn't want to hear. "I don't know. I guess as long as it takes to get her back on her feet."

"Any idea how long that will be?"

Her frown deepened. "The surgeon she just saw said it would be six to eight weeks of recovery."

Six to eight weeks? How the fuck would I make it without her that long?

Shit.

"I'll go with you. We'll leave tonight." It was the only logical solution I could come up with.

She shook her head. "No, Noel. You can't. There are a string of shows you're booked for. Maybe when you get done —"

"No. I can't be without you." The thought of not seeing that angel face everyday was a weight that nearly crushed me.

"You aren't coming with me."

I flinched. "You don't want me there?"

"Of course I do."

"Then what's the problem?" She wasn't making any sense.

"I won't hold you back from your dream. Finish this tour. I'm not going anywhere this time. I promise."

She was right. A lot of people were counting on us. The roadies and production people didn't get paid if we didn't play. I couldn't be selfish in this situation, even though I really, really wanted to.

"Okay, fine. But can I spend every off day I have with you?"

"I can't let you spend all that money flying back to see me every spare moment you get."

"Money isn't a problem for me, Lane. You know that. All that matters to me is being with you every second I can."

She sighed and reached her dainty fingers up to touch my face. "Sometimes you seem too good to be real."

I stared into her green eyes and threaded my fingers into her dark hair. "Now you know exactly how I feel about you."

Chapter 10

The bus felt cold without her. I lay on the bed and stretched my hand over to touch the pillow where her head typically laid. It'd only been a couple hours, and I was already losing my shit.

It was early, and I wasn't tired, but I didn't feel much like being social.

I picked up my cell and checked the time. In about ten minutes, her plane would land, and I could call and make sure she got there safe. Traveling alone wasn't something I liked her doing. There were too many crazies out there, and I wouldn't be there to shield her from them.

A knock on the door startled me from my thoughts. "Come in."

Riff pushed the door open and stood in the doorway. "We're about to start a *Halo* campaign. You in?"

This felt like old times—the bus rolling down a lonely stretch of highway while we kicked each other's asses in a war

115

video game. It was the best way we found to pass the time, other than sleeping, when we were cooped up inside Big Bertha for hours on end.

But right now, I wanted to wallow in my sadness over being without Lane. "Nah, I'm pretty tired."

Riff folded his arms across his chest while his crazy Mohawk stood high on the top of his head. "Dude, I know you miss her, but you can't mope around in this room the entire time she's gone. It's not healthy."

I sighed. "I know, but it's hard to be without her."

He nodded. "I know what you mean, but still you have to live, man. She won't be gone for ever."

That was true. I would see her again in a week when I got a three-day break between shows, but until then, I didn't see anything wrong with a little depression. "I get it. But I'm really just tired. It's been a long day."

A sarcastic laugh tumbled from his mouth. "Kyle took you shopping all day, how stressful could that be?"

Since he was my best friend, I needed to share with him my true venture of the day, so I fished the ring box from my pocket. "It was kind of a big deal."

I held it between my thumb and index finger for Riff's inspection.

His eyes widened. "Holy shit! Does she know you have that?"

I shook my head. "Nope." I sighed. "She left before I got a chance to ask her."

"That's a huge deal. You sure about this? Don't you think you should wait awhile?"

"No. It's the right time. It's something I've thought about doing since high school. Plus, that douchebag, Striker, keeps sniffing around her. What better way to show him she's off the market?"

Riff took the box and opened it up and let out a low whistle. "Well, don't rush in because you feel threatened by Striker. She loves you. Any idiot can see that."

That was what I thought too, but apparently Striker was the only blind man around. "Like I said, it's not just for his benefit. This is something I want. I want her to know I'm committed to her."

He handed me back the box. "If you're sure, then I'm happy for you. Now, get your ass up, and come help me whoop Trip's ass. I'm not taking no for an answer. I need my wingman."

I sat up and tucked the box back in my pocket, a little less heavy-hearted, and readied myself for some guy time.

An hour and a half into the game my cell rang. I checked the I.D. and felt a little silly for the sheer amount giddiness that rolled inside me from seeing Lane's name. I hoped the guys didn't notice. I'd never hear the end of it.

I pressed the phone to my ear after I rubbed my thumb over the green answer button. "Hey."

"God, I miss you." It was awesome to hear she was feeling the exact same way I did. "A week is so long."

"Too long," I agreed.

"Well, maybe I'll actually get some work done this week without you here to distract me all the time."

I laughed. "So glad you're looking forward to being without me."

"You know what I mean," she chided. "It'll be nice to have my proposal done for Striker this week."

The name Striker coming from those beautiful lips was just plain wrong. "Let's not talk about him."

"Noel…" Her voice held a warning.

"I'm not jealous or anything. I just don't like him." Honesty was the best policy about my thoughts that revolved around him.

Normally I would never have believed Lane would've gone for a guy like that, but after that night in the bar, I knew different. It was hard to get the vision of how he touched her that night when they danced out of my head. I snapped when I saw he was about to kiss her, and she was going to let him. Things in me went crazy and I attacked him to keep that from happening.

Lane sighed into the phone. "Okay, no more talk about him."

"Thank you." I paused. "Have you made it to the hospital yet?"

"I just pulled in the parking lot and wanted to call you before I went inside to tell you that I love you and miss you already."

The heart in my chest swelled. "I love you, too. Tell your mom I hope she gets back on her feet soon. I want to show her my mad pancake flipping skills."

She laughed. "Will do."

After the call ended, I felt better about missing her somehow. It gave me comfort to know I'd be with her soon and that I could call her anytime I wanted.

****

The next show was in Orlando, and it was an outdoors. Singing to a sold out crowd of over twenty thousand people always got me amped. It was still surreal at times that we had the amount of fans we did. And man, some of them were dedicated.

Backstage I watched as Embrace the Darkness ended their set. It was really starting to get under my skin that Striker and his band were getting a lot of notoriety.

He seemed to really enjoy hoarding on things that were mine—fans and Lane—things that meant the most to me.

Striker sauntered off the stage with that cocky grin he wore half the time I saw him. "Try not to chase the fans off, too," he commented as he walked past me.

I narrowed my eyes. "What the fuck is that suppose to mean?"

He spun on his heel to face me. "It means you're really good at driving things away. Careful, mate, or you'll drive more than your fans straight to me."

I closed the gap between us. "Try something with her, fucker. Give me one more reason to beat your ass."

He laughed. "You don't scare me, Falcon. I'm just waiting for you to fuck up before I make my move on Lane. She's too good for you."

Every muscle in my body shook and spots clouded my vision. On instinct, my fist drew back ready to blast Striker in his smug face.

My arm snapped forward, stopping inches from my target. I jerked my arm hard, so caught up in my anger I didn't notice Riff had my arm hooked in his.

Riff dragged me back. "He's not worth it."

My nostrils flared, and my brain couldn't absorb his words. "He needs to stop trying to fuck my girl."

Striker laughed as he stalked off, my heart still hammered hard as every piece of me still wanted to tackle him with full force.

Riff shoved me back. "Noel, dude, calm the fuck down. He's just trying to get to you and you're letting him. This is exactly what he wants—you to doubt Lane and drive her straight to him. Don't let that happen. Lane loves you."

My chest heaved as my body was still in fight mode. "You're right."

I scrubbed my hands down my face and took a deep breath. Striker found my weakness, and he took full advantage of it.

Trusting Lane wasn't the issue, but knowing Striker was set on taking her from me ramped me up even more to stake my claim on her for the world to see.

Chapter 11

After two weeks of being without Lane, I still missed her like crazy. Life just wasn't the same without her.

I rolled over and I picked up my cell and searched out her number. I needed her voice to be the first thing that I heard in the mornings. It was our new morning call routine and it was one of the only things that kept me going.

It rang a couple times before Lane's groggy voice answered. "Hey."

"Hey, baby. I didn't wake you, did I?"

"Oh, no. I was awake."

My brow furrowed. "What's wrong?"

"I'm feeling a little sick again," she answered.

"Are you having the same symptoms as before?" I questioned again.

"I wish." She sighed. "I've been sick to my stomach all morning."

I rubbed some sleep from my eye. "You've been throwing up?"

"Yeah, but thank God I was able to bring Mom home after surgery last night. It would've been hell to feel like this at the hospital."

I sat up in bed and then tossed my legs over the edge. "I'm coming down there."

"Noel, you have shows to do."

I shook my head even though she couldn't see me and hopped out of bed. "To hell with the shows, Lane. You need me, I'm coming down."

My suitcase was out on the bed before I even finished my last sentence.

"I'm fine, really." She was trying to convince me, but I knew she needed me. Kathy needed help getting around after her surgery, and Lane wouldn't be much help to her if she wasn't a hundred percent herself.

"I'm taking the next flight in what ever city we're closest to."

"Noel—"

"No more arguing about this, Lane. I want to come. Please don't fight me." I threw some clothes in the bag and zipped it up.

"Okay." I could hear the reluctance in her voice but pumped my fist anyway.

"I love you, and I'll see you soon," I told her before I ended our call.

I carried my luggage to the front of the bus and dropped it near the steps. Riff and Tyke sat at the table eating breakfast, while Trip stood at the island finishing up a bowl of cereal.

Riff eyeballed my bag before he turned his gaze on me. "What the fuck is that?"

I shrugged and knew this wasn't going to go over well with the guys. "I have to go, man."

"Go where?" Trip asked wiping milk from his lip after slurping down what was left in his bowl.

"He's going to Texas to be with Lane," Riff answered.

"What about the rest of our shows?" Tyke asked with a frown on his face.

"We'll have to cancel or postpone them, I suppose." All three of my band mates stared at me like I'd grown a third eye. "Guys, I'm sorry, but she needs me for a week or so. Her mom broke her leg, and she's sick. I have to go."

Riff flexed his jaw muscle, clearly pissed at my decision. "Fine. If you want to disappoint all the fans because you're being selfish—"

"Selfish? This is the first time in my life I'm thinking of others." I met each one of their stares individually. "I love her, guys. I have to be there when she needs me. I would really appreciate a little understanding on this."

After a couple tense moments of silence, Riff rubbed his chin. "I guess pushing back the dates a couple weeks wouldn't kill anybody." Trip and Tyke nodded in agreement. "I'll work on having them change the dates. It won't be easy, and will be a total pain in my ass, but I'll do it. Go take care of things."

A grin crept up on my face. "Thanks guys, I'll owe you one."

I instructed the bus to turn off at the next exit before I went back and to wake Kyle, who was still fast asleep in his foxhole to tell him I needed a ride.

In just a few short hours, I would see Lane again. The thrill of it excited me more than the biggest rush of playing live music to thousands of screaming fans.

Four hours later, I landed in Houston and picked up my rental car. The solitary drive was a nice change. It was very rare now-a-days to be completely alone. The silence was welcomed.

When I pulled into the driveway of Lane's childhood home, old memories of when we were in high school flooded me. I'd pull into this drive and honk my horn. Lane would come bouncing down the walkway and would hop in the passenger seat of my Chevelle. That was when life was simple.

I knocked on the front door, and Lane answered the door with a huge smile. "Hey!"

She was cheerful. A complete change from when I talked to her on the phone a few hours ago. "Feeling better?"

"Much! I don't know what was wrong with me this morning. I couldn't stop throwing up and every smell made me nauseous."

I grabbed her hand and pulled her outside with me, out of earshot of her mother. Alarms were going off like crazy in my head. "Do you think you're pregnant? It's been nearly four weeks since you saw that little munchkin looking doctor. It's possible."

Lane flinched. "No. I'm on birth control."

"It's not uncommon for birth control to fail if someone is on an antibiotic," I told her.

She tilted her head and crunched her brow. "How would you know that?"

I shrugged and I felt my cheeks burn in my embarrassment. "I read up on pregnancies a lot when I thought I was going to be a father. As you know, there's not much to do on that bus. A man can only stomach video games so long. Well, most men, anyway. The twins are addicted to them. So, I thought I would educate myself on babies."

She dropped her head. "What would we do if that's why I was sick this morning?"

I tipped her chin up with my index finger so she'd look at me. "We'd get married of course."

She pulled away. "You can't marry me because you feel guilty if I'm pregnant. I'm not Sophie."

"Hey." I wrapped my arms around her waist. "What we have is real. Sophie doesn't even exist on your level. A baby for us wouldn't be a bad thing."

She shook her head. "I still wouldn't want you to ask me solely because of it though. This isn't the 1800s. We can have a baby and not marry."

The temptation to dig the ring out of my luggage was overwhelming. If I gave it to her now, she'd never believe I'd had it before there was even a possibility of a baby. She would think I bought it on the way down here because I suspected she was pregnant after the way I had just jumped to the conclusion right off the bat.

I would just have to wait and plan out a beautiful proposal to make things perfect. She needed to know we could be perfect together and my reasoning for wanting to get married came straight from the heart.

She laid her head against my chest. "Now curiosity is killing me. Do you mind sitting with Mom while I run to the drugstore to buy a test?"

I ran my fingers through her dark hair. "Sure."

A half an hour later, Lane returned from the drugstore with a plastic bag in her hand. While she snuck off to the upstairs bathroom to take the test, I drummed my fingers on the arm of the couch and watched television with her mom. It was hard to believe the balance of my life would be determined by a ten-dollar test.

"Noel!" Lane called from upstairs.

I swallowed hard. "I'll be right back, Kathy."

I took the steps two at a time as I raced up to Lane. She waited in the doorway of her room. After she yanked me inside her bedroom, she plopped down on her bed. Tears filled her eyes before they rolled down her cheeks.

I instantly dropped to my knees in front of her and took her hand in mine. "Whatever it said, it's going to be okay."

She sniffed and batted away a couple tears. "You think a baby bed will fit on that tour bus?"

"Oh my God." I wrapped my arms around her waist. It was true, we probably weren't ready for this, but it didn't change the fact I was excited about the news.

I bit my lip and pulled back. I took her left hand in mine and peered up at her. "Lane, will you marry me?"

She shook her head. "No. I told you I won't marry you just because of a baby. This is just a decision on a whim for you. I don't want you to regret asking me or resent me later in life." She stood up, leaving me still kneeling on the floor by her bed.

"Where are you going?"

She stopped just short of walking out the door. "I need time to think and adjust to this news."

Watching her walk out and tell me no to one of the biggest dreams I'd ever had nearly crushed me.

I needed advice, and since I couldn't ask Lane for it, I went to my go-to person. I pulled my cell from my pocket and dialed my mom's number.

"Hi, honey. How are you?" Mom answered.

"I'm in need of some advice, actually. You got a minute?"

"All the time in the world for you. What's up?"

I cleared my throat as I stood and walked over to the window. The dock was in perfect view from here. My hand pressed against the warm glass when I saw Lane at the end of it looking out over the lake. It hurt me to know she was sad and didn't take my proposal seriously.

"Noel, you still there?" Mom's voice snapped me out of my thoughts.

"Sorry, Mom, I'm here. I need your help. I want to plan the perfect proposal for Lane," I said.

A giddy laugh echoed through the phone. It had been a long time since I'd heard Mom laugh like that. "I'd be honored to help. What do you have in mind?"

From there I broke into the entire story of how Lane and I reunited and how we were nearly torn apart by Sophie's lies. I didn't have to explain why I loved her so much to Mom. She knew. She always knew. I remembered how she would tell me how much she liked Lane and couldn't wait until the day she officially became part of the family.

The only thing I couldn't tell her was about the baby. Not because I didn't want to, but because I didn't feel right telling people before Lane was comfortable about the idea of letting our families know.

"So you'll help me? Lane is taking Kathy for a follow-up appointment tomorrow, so we'll have to work quickly."

"We'll decorate the dock and make it the most romantic thing she's ever seen. There's no way she won't take you seriously after we're done," she gushed. "I'll email you a list of everything you need to buy tomorrow. Just call me when you're ready for me to come over to help."

Chapter 12

The dock was quiet, and I knew I only had about three hours or so to pull all this together while Lane took her mother for a follow-up appointment at the hospital. I set the boxes and bags down on the wooden planks and went back to retrieve more supplies. The Escalade was crammed full of decorations. Mom's list was nuts, and it cost me a shit-ton of money for all of this, but it was worth it. It almost felt like Christmas. I couldn't wait to see the look on Lane's face when the dock was adorned in a massive amount of flowers and soft-glowing candles. She'd know what I was doing the moment she saw it.

Pulling a massive box out the trunk, a voice stopped me dead in my tracks. "Hello, son. Need a hand?"

I swallowed hard at the sound of my father's voice, and my entire body stiffened in preparation for the argument I knew was about to happen.

I leaned back with the box in hand. "No thanks. I'm pretty good at taking care of myself these days."

My father flinched and satisfaction shot through me knowing my words had the possibility of hurting him just as much as his did to me. "Son, please. Can we talk?"

I shook my head and turned to take the box down to the deck. I didn't have time to do this now. Out of all the opportunities for him to speak to me, he chose now? On the biggest fucking day of my life?

I set the box down and turned around, nearly colliding with Dad as he set the box he carried down beside mine.

He wasn't taking the hint to get lost. I folded my arms across my chest and stared at him expectantly. He hadn't changed too much since the last time I saw him over four years ago. His height matched mine, but his build was slighter. The hair on his head was clean cut just as I remembered, only now it was salt and pepper versus the dark color I was used to seeing. That was the only sign of aging I saw on him.

Dad shoved his hands on his hips, clearly uncomfortable. "Look, Noel, I know when we last saw each other, things ended on a bad note. I said some things—things I should've never said —and I'm sorry."

I rolled my eyes as a sarcastic laugh that I couldn't stop escaped my lips. "You're sorry? For what? Making the mistake of having a son that is only a disappointment to you? Because really, I got it the first time. I don't need you to come back and tell me again."

Dad ran his hand through his hair. It was a trait I picked up from him when we didn't know what to say next. "I was an asshole. I just didn't want you to throw your life away and I was angry. I shouldn't have said that, and there's not a day that goes by that I don't regret saying that to you."

Those were the words I had longed to hear him say for four fucking long years. I held his unwavering gaze. He meant what he said. I threw my head back and closed my eyes. His apology rang in my ears. "Why now?"

A ragged breath of his filled the silence. "Because I wanted to do it in person. I wanted to make sure you'd hear me out. When your mother told me about your project here today, I figured this was the perfect time to get you alone, and I hoped you'd listen to me."

I opened my eyes and stared at him, unsure of what to say in return.

"You don't have to accept it. It was harsh, and I've hated myself everyday for saying it to you." He took a tentative step towards me. "But I want you to know I didn't mean it. You're not a disappointment. If anything, I'm a disappointment to myself."

Dad was just as hot-headed as I was. Matter of fact that was where I got my temper from. Quick mouths were an undeniable trait in the Falcon gene pool. God knew I said so many things I didn't mean in my life in the heat of anger. I'd ask for forgiveness from Lane for the very same thing in the past few weeks. It would've been totally hypocritical to deny my father the chance to prove he was sorry, wouldn't it?

I bit my lip and nodded, agreeing with my own internal thought. Before I could say a word, Dad grabbed me into a huge hug, nearly squeezing the life out of me, taking my head gesture as a sign of acceptance.

I stiffened, but once inside his embrace, memories of the last time he hugged me flooded my brain. Graduation day—he was so proud. Both he and Mom knew what a struggle school had been for me growing up with dyslexia, so to them, it was huge that I had made it to that day. That was the last time my father said anything positive to me. He told me he was proud to be my father, which is why, I guess, it stung so much more when he called me a disappointment.

My eyes burned as tears threaten to spill out of them. Dad gripped me tightly one last time before he patted my back and pulled back. I was surprised to find him wiping moisture from his own eyes. I sniffed and batted away a couple tears of my own.

"I bet we look like a couple of pansies, huh?" he joked. It was his way of lightening mood.

I laughed at his lame attempt to be funny, and it felt good. "Yeah, we probably do."

He rubbed the back of his neck and peered down at the boxes by our feet. "I guess we should get busy. Your mom told me about your grand plan for this place tonight. You think you're finally ready to take the leap with Lanie? Marriage is a huge commitment."

I nodded confidently and was glad noise filled the empty space between us. "I've never been more ready for anything in my entire life."

Dad smiled and gave my shoulder a manly squeeze. "Guess we better get busy then."

We worked until nearly sundown. For a while, I doubted if it would even be possible to pull this off, but luckily, Mom came over and coordinated Dad and me on the decorations. Somehow, we had transformed the boat dock into a beautiful floral garden. It was something straight out of a movie with the archway of fresh flowers and gold and white fabric, tulle, and even more flowers covering every inch of the end of the dock— the spot Lane and I had spent so much time together. It was only right to ask her here. It brought our lives full circle here. This was the place of all our firsts, so asking her to be my wife here fit perfectly.

Mom finished lighting the last candle and I found myself mesmerized by the soft glow. Even as a guy, I could tell this was romantic. I sighed in contentment. Now it was just a matter of getting her out here.

Mom wrapped her tiny arms around my waist as we took in the sight of all of our handy work together. "It looks great, honey. Lanie is going to love this."

I gazed down at her and pulled her in for a tight hug. "Thanks, Mom, for everything."

"You're welcome, sweetheart." She pulled my head down and kissed my cheek. "I'm so proud of you."

Dad cleared his throat behind us. "Irene, we'd better go."

Mom nodded and gave me one last squeeze before letting go. "Will you come by tomorrow? I'd like for all of us to have a family dinner together. Bring Lanie, won't you? She's part of this family now, too."

I laughed. "She hasn't said yes, yet, Ma."

Mom waved her hands dismissively at me. "A technicality."

"We'll be there."

"Good." She smiled, clearly pleased with my answer.

Dad stepped forward and held out his hand. "Good luck, son. I'll see you tomorrow?"

"Tomorrow," I agreed.

With that, they both made their way up the path and back toward their house. The relationship with Dad wouldn't happen overnight. We'd have to work on it together. Everything in my life was suddenly starting to feel perfect. I had the woman of my dreams back in my life, a relationship that was finally on the mend with my parents, and a baby on the way.

The last thought would've scared a normal twenty-two year old guy, but not me. It almost made me giddy. Sure, we weren't exactly ready for a kid and the timing wasn't the greatest, but it was the perfect situation. I loved Lane with every inch of my being, and parenthood was something I couldn't imagine wanting to share with anyone but her.

A car door slammed shut, and I jerked my head towards the house. Lane and her mom must be back from town. My heart squeezed. On one hand I was so excited I felt as though I would burst, but on the other, fear caused my stomach to clench. What if she said no? Could I survive that?

I raked my fingers through my hair and made my way up the dock.

At the top of the hill, I noticed Lane helping her mother out of the car, and I felt a wave of panic like I'd never felt before. I ran over to the car.

Lane's eyes widened as I took over the brunt of Kathy's weight. "Noel! I've got this."

I shook my head vigorously. "Not today you don't. No lifting. I know that much."

A scowl filled her beautiful face. I knew she was pissed I was talking like this in front of her mother. She'd have questions. Lane said she wanted to wait to tell her Mom about being pregnant after she had an appointment with a physician, but I wasn't going to let her put herself at risk until she was brave enough to spill the beans. Maybe she was totally fine to help her mom out of the car, but dammit, that was my baby inside the love of my life. Neither of them was getting hurt on my watch.

I grabbed Kathy's arms and pulled her up to a semi standing position. "Scoot the wheelchair a little closer." My eyes snapped to Lane as a thought crossed my mind. "You didn't do this own your own at the hospital, did you?"

Lane shook her head. "No, I pulled up to the emergency room door and asked for someone to bring a wheelchair to help, like you said."

"Good." I turned my attention back to her mom. "Okay Kathy, on my count of three, I'm lowering you into the chair. One. Two. Three."

Once safely in the chair and with her casted leg positioned, I wheeled her up the ramp and into the house. Lane followed us inside, shutting the door behind her. The sun was just starting to set, leaving the room a little dark. I flipped on the light and then situated the wheelchair between the sofa and chair, directly in front of the television.

"Honey, do you mind getting me a glass of water and handing me the remote?" Kathy asked Lane.

Lane smiled and darted into the kitchen. Kathy cleared her throat the minute she left the room. "Are either of you going to tell me what's going on?"

I raised my eyebrows and sat down on the floral patterned sofa so I could look her in the eye. "What do you mean?"

She shook her head. "Don't play dumb with me. I've known you far too long for you to try to pull the wool over my eyes—either of you. When were you planning on telling me Lane's pregnant?"

I swallowed hard. Panic flooded me. I wasn't ashamed Lane was carrying my child. Hell, I was ready to tell the world, but if I let this secret slip before Lane was ready to tell her, I would never hear the end of it. The best plan I could come up with in those few seconds was to act dumb and clueless.

"What?"

Kathy let out a sarcastic laugh just as Lane emerged from the kitchen, glass in hand. "What's so funny?"

"Nothing," I answered quickly.

Lane raised an eyebrow at me and twisted her lips. "Nothing, huh? Didn't sound like nothing to me."

Desperate to get away from the situation, I stood and took her hand. "Let's take a walk."

Lane's gaze darted between me and her mother. "Oooookay?"

She knew something was up. I had to get her out of this room so I could tell her that Kathy was on to us. I tugged her towards the front door, but as soon as my hand reached the knob I heard her mom say, "Noel, we'll talk again later."

My shoulders tensed. Lane was just like her mom sometimes, relentless, so I knew we'd have to come clean to her tonight. She wouldn't let it go until we did. But I couldn't worry about that right now. Right now, I had bigger things on my mind

—like what this beautiful creature was about to say when I

asked her a very important question a few heartbeats from now.

Chapter 13

Lane's tiny hand fit perfectly inside mine. I held on tight to it as I led her around the backside of the house. Nerves inside my skin jittered. What I was about to do hopefully would change both our lives. All I needed was for her to say yes.

"What was that about in there? Did you say something to her?" Lane asked, breaking me out of my thought process.

"No. Nothing. But she knows," I answered.

"Why did you make such a scene at the car?"

I stopped and turned her to face me. "I'm sorry, but I was worried about you. Besides, Kathy's smart. I'm sure she would've picked up on it soon anyhow. She point blank asked me in there when we were going to tell her that you're pregnant."

Lane gasped and brought her hand to her mouth. "Oh my God. What are we going to tell her?"

She was starting to freak, so I had to reel her back in. I placed both hands on her shoulders and dipped my head, forcing her to look me in the eye. "Don't worry. We're adults. Things are going to be okay. If this would've been five years ago, yeah she might've given us some shit. They all would've. But this baby, it's part me and part you. Our families are going to love it."

A single tear slipped down her cheek, and I wiped it away with my thumb. "Things will be perfect, Lane. There's nothing we can't accomplish together, including raising our child together. Have faith in us."

She leaned her face into my palm, cupping it. "You really believe that?"

I nodded. "I do."

Lane threw her arms around my neck and pressed her tiny body against mine. "I love you."

"Forever," I whispered before I pressed my lips to hers.

She frowned when I pulled away and grabbed her hand again. "Where are we going?"

I bit my lip. "There's something down at the dock I want to show you."

When we came over the hill, I turned so I could watch Lane's expression when she saw what we had done earlier. Her eyes trailed down the dock, taking in the sight of the flower arrangements and candles lined up along the edges. The white rose petals sprinkled everywhere was the perfect touch, and I was glad Mom added that in.

"Noel...? You did all this?" she asked still not removing her eyes from the scene.

I cleared my throat. "Not totally on my own. I had some help."

"You did?"

I nodded. "Yep. Mom and Dad."

Her head whipped towards me. "Frank was here? Did you talk to him?"

I wrapped my arm around her shoulders and kissed her temple. "Yeah. We're working on things."

"That's fantastic news!" she exclaimed, peering up at me. "I bet that makes your mom happy."

"And me, too. It's hard to believe how much I actually missed him. This will be a good thing, especially now." I placed my free hand on her stomach. "Our kid should know all of his grandparents."

"Or *her* grandparents," Lane corrected.

I laughed. "Or *her*. Come on. There's more."

"More?" I could hear the skepticism in her voice.

I led her carefully down the hill, and once on the dock, I stooped down at the first arrangement and grabbed a single rose. It was a deep, rich red, and it reminded me of how deep she worked her love into my soul. Our love was eternal.

She smiled as she took it from my outstretched hand. "Oh, Noel. It's beautiful."

She put it to her nose and inhaled its luscious scent with her green eyes closed tight. "Yeah, you are."

She opened her eyes and grinned at me.

We walked together to the end of the dock where two chairs faced each other surrounded by candlelight. My Gibson guitar leaned against the railing, just waiting for me to carry out my plan. I held my hand out, gesturing for Lane to take a seat.

I sat across from her and picked up my guitar. She opened her mouth to protest, but I held up a finger to cut her off. "Before you say anything just hear me out. I've had this planned from the moment you came back to me. Our current situation has no effect on my feelings for you, other than making me love you even more. I had no idea it was possible to love someone so much. But I love you, Lane. You are the one for me. The only girl."

A few soft cords sounded as I strummed the cords to an acoustic version of *Only Girl* originally by *Rihanna* but sung in the style of *Boyce Avenue* because it fit my feelings for Lane perfectly. I sang about how she made me feel like a real man, and that she was the only one who was in control of me. I gazed into her green eyes and sang about making her my wife. She placed her fingertips to her lips as her eyes glistened.

The best part of the song was conveying that every moment with her meant everything to me. Singing was the best way I could get out everything I felt. Music spoke to my heart, and I knew from past experience it spoke to hers, too.

I bit my lip as emotions overcame my mind. The last verse came out, and I stopped strumming the guitar, completely lost in her eyes and the feelings I saw there. My voice softened as I got down on one knee in front of her and laid the instrument on the dock to continue the last chorus.

"You're the only one who understands." I took her left hand in mine and kissed each one of her knuckles, lingering on the one above her ring finger the longest. She was truly the only girl in the world for me.

A sniff from her drew my attention. Tears poured from her eyes, and my heart pounded in my chest unsure of what those tears meant.

"Lanie Vance, I have loved you from the moment I saw you. So many times I've dreamed of making you my wife one day, and I think today is that day. I love you with every inch of me. I'm drawn to your fire and passion, and I don't think I can ever be without it again. I want you everyday for the rest of my life. You and"—I leaned in and kissed her stomach and then my eyes met hers—"our baby. You two are my life. I've had this ring"—I pulled the princess cut diamond ring from my pocket —"since the day we went shoe shopping with Kyle. Before you knew you were pregnant. This had always been my plan. Having a baby doesn't change how I feel about you. You are my heart, Lane, always have been. Will you marry me?"

Her eyes searched my face, and I prayed to God she found whatever answer she was looking for when she stared at me. After what felt like an eternity, she nodded and a huge smile spread across my face. "Yes. YES!" Her fingers tangled in my hair, and she crushed her lips into mine. "I love you."

"Yeah?" I felt tears of exquisite joy slide down my face.

She cried and smiled at the same time. "Yes. I've always loved you."

"I knew you did, even when you fought it." She laughed, and I knew we were at the start of something really good.

I told her I loved her too before I wrapped my arms around her waist and kissed the sweet lips of my soon-to-be wife. This was it. This was what every up and down in my life had been bringing me to—this time and this moment with Lane.

"This is just the start to our forever," I whispered.

ROCK MY BED

(Black Falcon, #2)

Riff and Aubrey's story

Coming Soon

Michelle A. Valentine

Acknowledgements

First I want to thank you, the reader, without you writing would be meaningless. The love and support I feel from you guys drives me to keep writing. So, thank you, from the bottom of my heart.

Next comes my writing pals! You ladies truly inspire me and make me want to be a better writer. Thank you for talking me off the ledge many times and threatening to kick my ass when I get down. You three, Emily Snow, Katie Ashley, and Kelli Maine, mean the world to me and I am so unbelievably happy we've been through this crazy writing journey together. You guys are my eagle eyes. Thanks for everything you've taught me about the business over the years. Love you guys. GGBT foreva!

To Kristen Proby, I value our friendship and am so glad 2012 led you into my little smutty writing circle!

My new friends in the romance book blogging community, you know who you are. Thank you for pimping me and my work. I can't tell you how much I appreciate every Facebook share, retweet, post, review, author day and any way you've spread the word about my novels. You guys rock so much and are turning the publishing world upside down with your awesomeness! You guys are the life blood of all of us indie writers. We couldn't do it without you.

Tanya Keetch, aka THE WORD MAID, thank you for your keen editing eyes and always being there for me in a pinch. I am so thankful our paths crossed and am happy to call you a friend.

To Cris Soriaga Hadarly thank you for being one of the best readers EVER! Thank you for all the time and hard work you put into making fan trailers for this series. I can't tell you how many times I've watched them and just sat in awe of your mad ninja skills! Thank you for everything you do.

Holly Malgieri, my girl and one of favorite partners in crime. Thank you for all the laughs, interesting pictures and most of all for always putting together my book tours. I know how much work goes into coordinating them, and I want you to

Michelle A. Valentine

know I appreciate every minute you've spent on it. You rock, girlie!

My girls in Rock the Heart Discussion group, you all make me smile every day! Thank you for all your love, support and friendship.

Last, but never least, a huge thank you to my family. Thank you for putting up with an empty refrigerator, piles of dirty laundry and me hiding away until this novella was done. You guys are the best, and I couldn't/wouldn't do this without you. Love you lots.

Books by Michelle A. Valentine

The Black Falcon Series:

Rock the Heart

Rock the Band

Coming Soon: Rock My Bed

The Collector Series:

Demon at My Door

About the Author

*New York Times* and *USA Today* Best Selling author Michelle A. Valentine is a Central Ohio nurse turned author of erotic and New Adult romance novels. Her love of hard-rock music, tattoos and sexy musicians inspires her sexy books.

Facebook:

http://www.facebook.com/pages/Michelle-A-Valentine/477823962249268?ref=hl

Twitter: @M_A_Valentine

Blog:

http://michelleavalentine.blogspot.com/

Rock the Band

23753335R00089

Made in the USA
Lexington, KY
22 June 2013